LIEBERMAN'S CHOICE

CHOICE

Stuart Kaminsky

IVY BOOKS • NEW YORK

Ivy Books
Published by Ballantine Books
Copyright © 1993 by Stuart Kaminsky

Library of Congress Catalog Card Number: 92–40797

ISBN 0–8041–1176–6

This edition published by arrangement with St. Martin's Press, Inc.

Manufactured in the United States of America

First Ballantine Books Edition: April 1994

10 9 8 7 6 5 4 3 2 1

To the members of the Liars Club,
who can't resist going to the edge

"Not till I know what's happening right here.
Not till the keepers of the inner shrine have
answered me. How. You inside. Unbar the
door. Is the king there? Tell him to hurry. Tell
him a soldier's out here with bad news."
—EURIPIDES, Iphigeneia in Tauris

1

The midnight waves scratched silver fingers along the narrow beach at the end of the street. Through the open window of his car, Bernie Shepard heard the waves and the rush of traffic half a block behind him on Sheridan Road. He parked next to a fire hydrant, picked up his shotgun, opened the car door, and stepped into the night. The dog leaped out after him, silent except for the pad of his paws on the street.

It was mid-September. The moon was full and the waves hitting the Chicago shore of Lake Michigan were sluggish and cold. And in spite of their moonlit silver caps, dirty. No more than a month ago, at the end of this street, Shepard had watched the uneatable coho salmon flop around, mating, dying just off the shore.

Shepard and the dog were alone.

Only the drunk and drugged, only the incautious homeless, only those whose late night shifts require it walked the streets of low rises and two-flats on Fargo and the other nearby streets that ran a single block from Sheridan to the lake. These were streets that twenty years ago had been respectable, thirty years ago had been choice, and forty years ago had been elite.

Now the old people who lived here went to bed early and double-locked their doors. The professionals who found the neighborhood a bargain treated their lives like a movie, believing and disbelieving the danger at the same time.

Shepard and the dog crossed the street to the Shoreham Towers. The Towers stood fifteen stories high. There was

1

nothing in sight for five blocks in any direction that rose higher in the cloudless sky than this 1930s rectangle of red brick and white ledges.

Shepard opened the outer door of Shoreham Towers and entered. He made no attempt to hide the weapon in his hand. Fifteen years ago, the lobby of the Shoreham had a carpet and chairs. They were long gone. The chairs had been stolen, the carpet taken up by management before it too was taken.

The lobby smelled of disinfectant and the memory of that damp carpet. On the walls were faded prints—pink flowers and ornate tropical birds—protected by dusty glass.

He moved to the inner lobby door, opened it with a key, and stepped in. The inner lobby still had a few chairs, a trio of artificial plants that looked artificial, and an overhead light fixture with eight teardrop bulbs, one of which flickered on and off as the man and dog moved into the open elevator.

The dog sat and watched as the man pushed a button and the elevator doors closed. The elevator lurched, still half asleep, sluggishly upward 1-2-3-4-5-6-7-8-9-10. The elevator stopped with a grunt of steel and the doors opened.

Shepard, dog behind him, headed down the corridor of the tenth floor and stopped in front of an apartment. He listened. There was a faint sound of voices behind the door. Shepard opened the door slowly, very slowly with a key and stepped into the darkness touched by the moonlight through the windows and a thin slice of yellow light coming from the partly open door of the bedroom in front of him. The dog entered and watched Shepard carefully close the door to the apartment.

The voices were clearer now, a man and a woman. Shepard moved silently to the bedroom door and stood listening.

". . . to be safe," the woman said.

Shepard motioned to the dog, who understood, pushed the bedroom door open with a paw, and trotted in silently.

"I checked. He's on an all-night stakeout on the South Side. There's no way . . ."

The man stopped suddenly, midsentence. He had seen the dog.

Shepard kicked open the bedroom door and raised the shotgun. He had heard others tell the tale, claiming moments like this were gauzy dreams, slow motion. But he sensed none of this.

Andy Beeton was throwing off the blanket. He was naked. He reached for a gun in a holster draped over a chair near the bed. Shepard fired. The blast sprayed Beeton with red-black dots against his pale skin and spun his head to the right, taking his left eye. He was dead before he slumped against the night table, tipping the table lamp to the floor and bringing down the nearby chair and holster with his outstretched hand.

Somewhere behind Shepard, the dog made a sound, not quite a whimper, maybe even a yawn.

Shepard turned to the woman, who had sat up, not bothering to cover her breasts. She was small and wide-eyed. Her nipples were dark and pointing at him. Her long hair tumbled over one eye. Her head shook "no" slowly and her mouth formed the word *no* as Shepard fired and turned away, not wanting to see what the blast did to her. But as he took a step back to the door, she made a sound, an almost cooing sound. He turned to see what he did not want to see and knew that the sound was only a memory and that Olivia was dead.

There was no more to look at or do here. He reloaded the shotgun and snapped his fingers. The dog looked from him to the bed and back again before obeying the sound and moving into the darkened living room.

Before Shepard and the dog had crossed the living room, they could hear voices in the corridor.

"What happened?"

"What was that?"

"Where did it come from? I think it was . . ."

"I'm calling the police."

"Jerry, mind your own business."

"I'm calling the police, Flo. You hear what I'm saying here? Someone could be for Chrissake dead or . . ."

Shepard stepped through the apartment door and into the corridor. The dog trotted in front of him. He reached back and closed the door.

"Mr. Shepard, what ha . . . ?"

The speaker was a short, fat man with gray hair that had gone electric wild in his sleep. He was wearing a gray robe. He had stopped speaking when he looked first at Shepard's face and then at the gun at Shepard's side.

There were two other men and two other women in the hallway, all of them over sixty. Shepard and the dog strode toward the open elevator door, the people moving silently to the side, out of his way.

As Shepard and the dog entered the elevator, an apartment door opened and two men, both in their thirties, both a bit drunk, stepped out.

"What the hell's goin' on?" asked one of the men.

Shepard and the dog faced forward. As the doors closed one of the drunken men, the bigger of the two, looked at Shepard and the shotgun in his hand, took a step toward him, and then thought better of it. The elevator doors closed and Bernie Shepard could hear.

"What the fuck is goin' on out here?"

As the elevator lurched upward, the voices below faded in the distance and the grind of weary gears.

"I'm calling the cops."

"Jerry, mind your own business."

When the elevator reached the top, the fifteenth floor, Shepard and the dog stepped out into a silent corridor of locked apartments. Shepard moved to a door marked STAIR-WAY, pushed it open so the dog could step in ahead of him, and followed the animal into the dim-bulbed shadows.

Shepard did not think, did not allow himself to think. Images behind him in the apartment screamed for attention. He ignored them and climbed the stairs, listening to his footsteps clang and echo and howl back from fifteen stories below. At the top of the stairwell was a heavy metal door.

4

Shepard put down his gun and pushed the door open. Warm air rushed in.

Picking up the gun, Shepard stepped out onto the roof of the Shoreham Towers, commanded an unbidden image to go away, leaned the gun against the wall, and closed the door. A heavy metal bar rested against the wall next to where he had placed the gun. While the dog padded around the pebble-covered roof, Shepard, straining, slowly wedged the bar against the door. He tested it, found it firm, and retrieved his gun. Again he was aware of the sound of the waves, the rush of traffic. Nothing outside of the Shoreham Towers had changed in the last five minutes.

An empty water tower, its once orange body covered with graffiti, its four girderlike legs acned with rust, sat in the middle of the roof. Shepard moved toward the tower. Beneath it was a clearing of almost ten feet by ten feet surrounded by concrete blocks that Shepard had brought up one at a time, in the dead of night, over the past six weeks. In one corner of the minifortress was a formidable cache of weapons. Next to the weapons was a chest containing food. Atop the chest was a jug of water. Shepard stepped through a narrow passage between the blocks and checked the food, water, weapons, and a first-aid kit. He pulled out a blanket and a two-way radio, laid the radio on the blanket, and adjusted a rolled-up sleeping bag so that it rested against the blocks.

Satisfied, Shepard stepped back through the passage between the blocks and walked to the corner of the roof.

The dog came to his side, sat, and waited.

There would be no sirens. They would come silently, and if he wished, he could look over the edge of the tower down to the street to watch them come. They would ask questions, find the bodies, wait for orders, and gradually figure out where he was. It would take time. Half an hour. An hour. Time.

To the south, toward downtown, he could see the snake of car lights along Lake Shore Drive. The distant high rises along the drive were darkened but not fully asleep. Well beyond them he could see the downtown peaks, even the Sears Tower. Then Shepard looked toward the lake and saw darkness except for a dot of light that must have been a boat. To the north just a few blocks away, though it was too dark to see it, was the cemetery that divided Evanston and Chicago at the lakeshore. To the west lay the city, sleepily alight even at this hour.

Shoreham Towers was in East Rogers Park, not a melting pot, but a scared puzzle of Haitians, Jamaicans, poor Southern whites, Mexicans, Puerto Ricans, Indians, Pakistanis, recent Russians. Fifteen blocks to the west was West Rogers Park, small homes, threatened, mostly Jews with odd pockets of Chinese and slightly more affluent Russians.

Shepard turned from the edge of the roof. The odds were good, he knew, that they would send Lieberman. And behind him would come Kearney. It was Kearney's district now. But now lasted only an instant.

Shepard went back into his concrete-block stockade with the dog behind him, leaned his back against his rolled-up sleeping bag, and closed his eyes.

2

When the call came a little after two in the morning, it did not wake Abraham Lieberman, nor did it awaken his wife, Bess, but for different reasons.

Bess had learned three decades earlier to sleep with thirty-six-decibel ear plugs to block out the snoring of her husband. Each year, Abe snored less, not because the problem had passed but because he slept less.

On this early morning, wearing his favorite green robe with hardly a bit of nap remaining on its threadbare surface, Abe sat in the kitchen with the door closed doing the *New York Times* crossword puzzle and drinking an iced mixture of diet cola and coffee. He considered shaving.

There were four prevailing opinions about the appearance of Abraham Lieberman. Bess thought he looked like Harry James. The Alter Cockers, the regulars at his brother Maish's deli on Devon, after much and continuing debate led by Syd Levan, thought he looked like a dyspeptic dachshund, while at the Clark Street Station out of which Lieberman worked, he was accepted as the Rabbi, which only his partner called him, or the Bloodhound, a title settled upon him by a well-educated car thief more than a dozen years ago not because of any particular tenacity on Lieberman's part but because of the policeman's sober face and lean, round-shouldered body.

Lieberman was well aware that he was not an imposing figure at five seven and hovering around 145 pounds. He looked, even to himself, a good five years older than his sixty years. Bess thought his best features were his curly gray hair and his little white mustache. Lieberman could never see anything in his mirror except his own long-dead father in disguise.

Bess was five years younger than Abe. On a bad day she looked fifteen years younger. On a good day she looked like his daughter. She was no beauty, but she was a lady. The daughter of a South Side butcher, she carried herself like Katharine Hepburn. The Alter Cockers admitted without reservation that Bess had "class."

Over the past few years it was always something different that seemed to wake Lieberman up each morning between four and five. Usually it was a sound, a real or imagined movement by Bess, his own snoring, an inner clock that had gone wrong just after his fifty-seventh birthday, or a memory. This morning it was different, a dream.

Lieberman was not a dreamer. He knew that everyone dreamed, but he was not usually moved by his dreams nor did he particularly remember them, but this one had been different.

A face had loomed before him suddenly. A round white face with sunken dark eyes, a face not attached to a body. The mouth of the face had opened to reveal red gums and no teeth. The tongue was white and moving, and a word was whispered and then another. "They will die."

He knew the face. The face was telling the truth, but the face was a balloon. If he could wake up, unlock the night table drawer with the key around his neck, get out his gun, and fire at the balloon, it would burst. He knew it would splatter blood on Bess, on him, on the new flowered comforter, but if he didn't destroy this balloon, someone would die.

Abe had forced himself awake with a grunt and sat up in bed.

He knew the face. Frankie Kraylaw. It was a face, a smiling, innocent face that had troubled him from time to time more than once over the last four months during his waking hours. Now it was intruding on his dreams.

Lieberman had listened to Bess's even breathing and then had gotten out of bed. He had tiptoed out of the room and retrieved his book of *New York Times* Sunday crossword puzzles, an early birthday gift to himself. He would be sixty-one at the end of the month, the twenty-ninth. The prospect did not please him.

The puzzle, Lieberman found himself working on was unusually difficult or he was unusually tired. He wasn't getting it. What he was getting was a stiff neck from sitting in the same position at the kitchen table. Dawn and a hot shower would help.

Above him he heard Lisa's bed creak. If she walked across the floor, he would leave his puzzle, leave his drink, and pad as quickly as he could to the bathroom. He was not ready for another session with his daughter, who had left her husband and moved back into her parents' house on Birchwood Street in West Rogers Park with her two children, Barry and Melisa. Lisa was an endless vacillation between uncertainty and determination. If Lieberman even suggested that her husband, Todd Cresswell, was not a self-serving monster, she would give him a Talmud-length catalog of terrible deeds, none of which struck Lieberman as particularly terrible. If he, however, said something that might be construed as critical of Todd, she would point out her father's own imperfections, a remarkable talent she had developed at an early age.

It was sometimes best to avoid Lisa. This was certainly one of those times. When he heard her footsteps above him, he got up quickly, dumped the remains of his drink down the drain, leaving the glass in the sink, and took a step toward the door, puzzle page and pen at the ready, bathroom only eight feet away promising hot water and privacy.

That was when the phone rang.

Lieberman picked it up before it could ring a second time.

"Yes," he said.

"Abe, it's me. You awake?"

Hanrahan sounded sober and serious.

"I'm awake, Bill."

"You know the Shoreham Towers?"

"On Fargo, just off Sheridan. I think Bess has a cousin who lives there."

Lisa was definitely on the way down the stairs. He could hear the wooden steps creaking. Escape was no longer possible.

"Bernie Shepard lives here too. Looks like about an hour ago he came home, found his wife in bed with Andy Beeton, and blew them both to hell and back."

Lieberman said nothing.

He did not believe in prophetic dreams. He didn't disbelieve either. He would wait till he had gathered more evidence, and if the evidence did not come, he could live with the mystery. Less than an hour ago he had dreamed of Frankie Kraylaw, a man who had threatened to kill his wife. Perhaps he had dreamed it at the same moment Bernie Shepard had . . .

"Abe, you there?"

"I'm here, Bill. Kearney know?"

"No, you're the first to hear the pleasant tidings. Congratulations."

"I'll tell Nestor to find Kearney," said Lieberman. "I'll be there in twenty minutes." He hung up.

Lieberman knew them all, Shepard, his wife, Olivia, and Andy Beeton. Beeton, a detective out of Edgewater, he knew the least, but he vaguely remembered that Beeton was married and had a big wife. There was nothing else he could think of at the moment, pro or con, about Beeton. Bernie Shepard, however, was a story, a bull of a man about ten years younger than Abe, a man with a temper, a man no one really wanted to work with, but a man who everyone agreed was an honest, good cop. Bernie was the kind who volunteered for cleanups, who had a bad word to say about SWAT teams, who trusted no one, and got along with only one partner, Alan Kearney, who six weeks ago had become captain at the Clark Street Station and Lieberman's boss.

Shepard had married Olivia about ten years earlier. The story he heard was that Kearney had met her when she had been assaulted less than an hour after she got off the Greyhound from Muscatine, Iowa. He had helped her to find work, had introduced her to Bernie Shepard. Lieberman remembered her from Kearney's promotion party a few months ago. She had long hair and large eyes, and was shy. Lieberman remembered that, but her face wouldn't come to him. Instead of Olivia Shepard's face, he saw Jeanine Kraylaw, the young, frightened wife of Frankie Kraylaw about whom Lieberman had just dreamed.

Lieberman put down the phone and looked at Lisa as she opened the kitchen door and came in.

Lisa was wearing her pink robe with a frilly collar. Her dark hair was tied back. She looked pretty. She looked young and she looked miserable. From the day of her birth, the Liebermans' only child had been, in her father's opinion, "serious." She had been a beautiful child who took in everything and seldom laughed aloud. She had been a wonder student. She had gone to Mather High School and then to the University of Chicago, where she had met a serious young assistant professor of classics with a love of Greek tragedy. They had two children and lived, although Lieberman was not aware of it till a month go, discontentedly ever after.

"I'm hungry, but I don't want to eat anything," she said, moving past him to the refrigerator. "I get depressed and eat. I eat and I get fat and I hate myself. I'll look like Aunt Rose. I can't afford to look like Aunt Rose and hate myself right now. I can be a little displeased with myself, but not hate. I heard the phone ring."

"Yeah, I've got to make a call and go," he said,

watching her eye the contents of the refrigerator critically.

"A murder?" Lisa asked, reaching for a see-through bag of bagels Lieberman had brought home from Maish's.

"Yes," he said, dialing the station. "There's some cream cheese with chives at the back, on the second shelf."

Nestor Briggs answered the phone. Nestor always answered the phone at the Clark Street Station at night. Nestor liked to work nights and double shifts. Nestor did not like to go home. The only family Nestor had was an ancient one-eyed cat that Nestor called Sy Klops. Lieberman gave Briggs what he had and told him to track down Kearney.

When Lieberman hung up the phone, Lisa asked, "You think a little cream cheese with chives would be bad for me?"

"You're a biochemist," he said. "If you don't know . . . ?"

"Abe," she said, for she always used his first name when she was about to point out one of his many failings as a father, "do you know what I do? I mean what I do when I work?"

"Precisely?"

"Approximately."

"No," he admitted. "Enzymes elude me. I respect them and you, but their function is an enigma. I've got to go."

She put the bag of bagels and the white carton of cream cheese and chives on the kitchen table.

"Go," she said, pulling a knife from the dish drainer on the sink. "You need the *Times* puzzles?"

He dropped the book on the kitchen table and placed the pen on top of it.

"You can finish that one and do the next. That's it. You going to be all right?" he asked.

She sat, surveyed the snack, and shrugged.

"No. Maybe."

Lieberman walked to his daughter and leaned over to kiss the top of her head.

"You wanna talk later?" he asked.

"I'll talk to Mom. Go rid the streets of crime."

"I'll try to get back in time to take Barry and Melisa to lunch at Maish's," he said softly as he opened the door. His grandchildren were both asleep in the living room beyond. Barry, almost thirteen, was in his sleeping bag on the floor. Melisa, eight, slept in the pullout bed that had been a gift from Bess's father more than thirty years ago.

"It's a school day, Abe," Lisa whispered with a sigh, slicing a poppy seed bagel.

"I'll take them for ice cream tonight."

"Sounds fine," Lisa said, lifting the top off the cream cheese carton.

Fifteen minutes later, shaved, holster in place, Lieberman tiptoed past the closed kitchen door, through the living room, careful to avoid Barry on the floor, and out the door.

The night was warm but not really hot. Lieberman needed a coffee. Normally, he ground beans when he got up, but since Lisa and the kids had come, he had not only stopped grinding in the morning to keep from waking them up, but he had also avoided turning on the microwave to heat leftover Bavarian Creme because the microwave hummed and rang.

There was an all-night 7-Eleven run by Howie Chen's cousin or uncle next to a Sari shop near Western, and it was on the way to the Shoreham. Howie was the only non-Jew in the Alter Cockers who hung out at Maish's T&L on Devon. It was generally and incorrectly agreed among the Alter Cockers that every Chinese businessman in Rogers Park was related to or knew Howie and owed each of the Alter Cockers a discount.

Lieberman took a less direct route to the Shoreham down Broadway so he could stop at the White Hen Pantry near Argyle. There was no one in the parking lot of the White Hen when he pulled in. And there was no one inside but the morning shift clerk, a puffy-faced young woman in a white smock.

"Poli around?" Lieberman asked, going to the pots of coffee and pouring two into plastic cups.

"You kiddin'?" asked the young woman, who folded her arms and watched him put the lids on the cups. "He doesn't come in till eleven."

Lieberman brought his two cups of coffee to the counter.

Up close the woman had the pale waxen look of a tracker. The white jacket had long sleeves. He looked at her arms anyway long enough to be sure she was watching him. She didn't reach for her arms or hug herself or find something to do, which led Lieberman to the conclusion that she was probably clean.

"Kraylaw," he said, fishing out two dollars. "He still working here?"

"Kraylaw," she repeated ringing up the sale and giving him change. "The kid."

Frankie Kraylaw was almost thirty, but he looked like the friendly best buddy teenager in a "Brady Bunch" rerun.

"The kid," Lieberman agreed.

"No. I don't think so," she said as another customer, a man in a night watchman's uniform too warm for the weather, walked in and headed for the coffee.

"I'll check with Poli," said Lieberman, heading for the door.

"You a . . . ?"

"I am," said Lieberman.

"I heard the kid had some trouble with his wife or something."

"Yeah," agreed Lieberman.

"He's a creepy guy," the woman said with a look of distaste. "Not creepy like lots who come in here. Present company excepted, of course."

"Thank you."

"Creepy," she said, "Big smile on his face like Uncle Ira."

"Uncle?"

14

"Ira. In *Invasion of the Body Snatchers*. Nothing behind the smile like, like he was a puppet or something. Like . . ."

"Howdy Doody," he supplied.

"Who?"

Lieberman pushed the door open with his elbow as the weary night watchman poured coffee on himself and said, "Goddamn the hell."

Even if the streets hadn't been almost traffic-free, and he had gone straight there, it would have taken Lieberman only fifteen minutes to get to the Shoreham from his house.

He made it to the Shoreham in twenty even with the stop for coffee.

When Abe Lieberman had entered his kitchen in the hope of an insomniacal retreat of coffee and crosswords, his partner, William Hanrahan, had stepped into the Shepard bedroom.

Hanrahan was on nights because he had requested them, which meant he and Lieberman had been split for the month. Since Hanrahan had just come off sick leave after being shot during a murder investigation, the new captain, Kearney, had okayed the request without question.

Lieberman knew the reason for his partner's shift request. Hanrahan did not want to face the night. He could sleep during the day knowing that if he opened his eyes, there would be sun through his windows. It might be gray Chicago sun, but it would be sunlight and not the awful night loneliness.

Hanrahan had recently celebrated his fiftieth birthday, an event the details of which he had reported to Lieberman.

"I went to the Black Moon and Iris made me a Chinese birthday dinner, good stuff."

Hanrahan had been going with Iris Huang for more than two months. He had met her when he had a few too many drinks at the Black Moon while he was supposed to be watching the apartment of a hooker named Estralda across the street. Hanrahan's few drinks had probably gotten Estralda killed. Later, when Hanrahan had been shot, Iris had been at his hospital bedside almost every night after. And when he got out she had tended him at home. He had, as yet, not taken Iris to bed nor had he even asked her to spend the night.

"Well, Rabbi," he had told Lieberman, continuing about his birthday experience, "I'm eating, only customer in the place, a Thursday afternoon, mind you, and the music comes on, guy with a Chinese accent on a tape is singing 'Happy Birthday,' leaves the name out when he comes to it. Nobody sings my name, not even Iris. Her father's back in the kitchen. I don't think he knows my name or wants to. Who knows? Depressing as hell or what?"

Now, his birthday four weeks and two days behind, Bill Hanrahan, his cheeks pink, his dark hair cut short but just thick enough to cover the scar on his scalp where he had been shot, stepped into the Shepard bedroom. His handsome flat Irish face was a little puffy. His shirt, blue as always, was neatly pressed, as was his dark red tie. Bill had not had a drink since he went into the hospital, but what he saw now made him hope that Shepard had at least a beer in his refrigerator.

The young uniformed cop who stood off to the side of the bed, being careful not to step in blood or look at the corpses, said, "Neighbors say the guy who did it lives here, cop named . . ."

"Shepard, Bernie Shepard," Hanrahan supplied. "Ring any bells?"

"Oh shit," said the cop looking at the bodies, stunned. The young cop was about the age of Hanrahan's oldest son, Michael, who spoke to his father only when asked to do so by his mother.

"You got a way with words, son," said Hanrahan. "That's his wife and Andy Beeton, detective out of Edgewater."

"That's Andy B . . . ?"

"If you're gonna throw up and you can't hold it, the john's over there, through that door. Push it open with your

16

elbow. Use the toilet if there's nothing in it, flush it with your elbow and don't wash your hands."

"I'm okay," said the young cop.

"Sure you are," sighed Hanrahan. "You're okay and I'm okay. Get out in the hall and help your partner keep everyone out of here."

When the young cop left, Hanrahan forced himself to the bed. He avoided looking at what remained of Olivia Shepard, but Andy Beeton's one good eye looked at him with a question. He had no answer.

Bill Hanrahan was a lapsed Catholic who, with the help of Father Sam ("Whiz") Parker at Saint Bart's, was making some small efforts to find his way back. This night was not helping.

Hanrahan left the room and went back through the living room to the kitchen, opened the refrigerator door, considered a blasphemous thanks to the Virgin Mother, and pulled out a bottle of Molson dark. Then he opened the freezer door and let the frigid air tingle coolly against his face. Next he stepped back and let the door close. The beer bottle was cold. The beer bottle felt good. He put it back in the refrigerator and closed it.

What was the line he liked so much in *The Man Who Shot Liberty Valance*? Oh, yes, Edmond O'Brien, the town drunk who's been told by John Wayne that he can't have a drink, demands a beer saying, "A beer ain't drinking."

"First medicinal wine from a teaspoon. Then beer from a bottle," Hanrahan quoted aloud from *The Music Man*.

The Music Man was Maureen's favorite musical. When she had left, he had kept the album.

He opened the door again and took out the bottle of Molson.

The medics, lab crew, homicide—everyone would be coming as soon as he got on the phone. Television and radio crews, newspaper reporters, and who knew who else would be coming when the word got out that a cop had killed his wife and another cop. And someone, probably Sergeant William Hanrahan, would have to tell

17

Andy Beeton's widow before she got the news from a neighbor or her television set. Hanrahan tried to remember if Beeton and his wife had any kids. He also tried to remember if he had ever met Beeton's wife.

That was when he moved to the phone, considered using his handkerchief, muttered, "Shit," picked up the phone, and called Lieberman.

Alan Kearney had sensed the ringing in his sleep, had heard the low click that comes just before the first ring. Kearney had the phone in his hand before the first ring had ended. He was quick, but not quick enough. Carla Duvier stirred at his side, and he knew she was awake and listening.

He didn't bother to whisper into the phone.

"Kearney."

Carla, nude, model-thin with firm, ample breasts that looked natural but, Kearney knew, were not, rolled toward him and reached for his stomach with her eyes closed. Her hand glided down playing with the hair below his flat belly as he listened to Nestor Briggs and said, "I'll be there in half an hour. Yeah, I know where it is."

Kearney was forty-two years old, roughhouse good-looking with a broken nose and a reputation for common sense that had earned him the promotion and move to Clark Street.

Word out was Kearney was a comer, a guy to watch, well-connected, well-liked, and only weeks away from marrying Carla Duvier, whose father was D. Wayne Duvier. D. Wayne owned. How much he owned and where was speculation, but it was a great deal.

Kearney hung up as Carla's hand went between his legs.

"What's up?"

It was a familiar joke between them, but this time Kearney didn't respond. He sat up looking into the past, hearing Bernie Shepard's voice but not his words, seeing Olivia Shepard's face but not her eyes.

"A cop just killed a man and a woman."

Kearney removed her hand, kissed the palm, and then leaned over to kiss her lips before getting out of bed.

"Do you know him?" she asked, sitting up.

Kearney had both his underpants and trousers on before he answered, "Bernie Shepard."

3

The corridor in front of the Shepard apartment was crowded with tenants of all shapes, sizes, and ilks, more tenants than could possibly live on this floor. A young uniformed cop Lieberman recognized but whose name he didn't know was trying to get information from the crowd, all of whom were eager to provide opinions about the Shepards, Russia, Ross Perot, and politics in the city of Chicago.

Juggling the plastic foam cups of coffee he carried in each hand, Lieberman eased his way to the apartment. The door was slightly ajar. He pushed it open with his elbow. Standing a few feet in front of him, Bill Hanrahan was talking to a gray-haired old man in a robe who looked well beyond nervous.

"Father Murphy," said Lieberman, handing his partner a coffee. "They got a microwave? The coffee's getting cold."

Hanrahan nodded and looked at the gray-haired man.

"Thanks, Mr. Slovin. We'll get back to you."

Mr. Slovin looked at the partly open bedroom door.

"I can go?"

"You can go," Hanrahan said.

Slovin moved to the door.

"You want it open or closed?"

"Closed," said Hanrahan, and Slovin closed the door.

Hanrahan took both coffees and moved into the kitchen with Lieberman at his side.

"Lab's having a busy night. They're late, but Ryberg's here," said Hanrahan.

"Saw his car downstairs."

"Microwave," said Hanrahan, putting the coffees down and opening the microwave door.

"Give it two minutes. Make it hot."

Hanrahan complied.

"Anything else?"

"Yes," said Lieberman. "Kearney will probably be here soon."

"And?"

"And you've got alcohol on your breath."

"A beer. One beer. Look in that bedroom and then blame me, Rabbi."

Lieberman walked to the bedroom. Behind him the microwave pinged softly. Lieberman needed a nice quiet ping like that on his microwave. He pushed the bedroom door open. Ryberg, the medical examiner, and his assistant were examining the bodies. Ryberg looked back at Lieberman and smiled, a put-on smile. Ryberg was close to retirement, a thin gnarled man with arthritic knuckles.

Lieberman closed the bedroom door and turned around to face Hanrahan, who handed him a coffee.

"Jesus Christ," said Lieberman.

"My words exactly," agreed Hanrahan, sipping the black coffee. "Bernie did it. We're up to our asses in witnesses. I put a call out on him. Armed, dangerous. Old Rules-Is-Rules Shepard just broke every one of them. It's going to be a long night."

Lieberman nodded. The coffee was bitter.

"Abe, I have not been drinking. The beer is the first drink I've had. Would I lie to you?"

"No," said Lieberman. "You might lie to yourself."

"I've done that before, but I'm not doing it now."

The front door opened and a muscular black uniformed cop stepped in, holding an envelope at the corner with the tips of his fingers. The cop's eyes were dancing with discovery.

"Parnell?" asked Lieberman.

"Parnell," the black cop confirmed.

"Close the door," said Hanrahan as the crowd beyond gawked through the opening.

Parnell nodded and pushed the door closed with his free hand.

"Checked out a car parked across the street in front of a hydrant. I think it's Sergeant Shepard's. This envelope was on the front seat."

Lieberman took the envelope and set his half-finished coffee on the glass-topped table. Neat printed letters on the envelope said: TO THE DETECTIVE IN CHARGE OF THE SHEPARD CASE.

Lieberman showed the envelope to Hanrahan.

"Officer Parnell," Lieberman said, "can you go back to the car and see what else you can find without touching anything?"

Parnell nodded and left.

"Something bad is definitely coming," said Hanrahan. "We gonna wait for Kearney?"

Lieberman answered by opening the envelope, pulling out a sheet of thick paper, and reading.

"What's it . . . ?" Hanrahan began, but Lieberman cut him off by handing him the paper. There wasn't much written on it. He handed it back to Lieberman.

"Holy Christ. He's on the goddamn roof."

There were no sirens. Shepard hadn't expected any, but there were sounds on the street. Cars pulling up, voices. Soon, it would be soon. He sat motionless, a high-powered rifle in his lap. The dog looked at the barricaded metal door and growled.

"Quiet," Shepard said softly, and the dog was quiet. "I hear them."

Shepard checked his watch. It was twenty minutes to four. He got up and moved slowly across the roof to the door. Someone on the other side was turning the handle slowly, carefully. Then a push that didn't even shake the door.

"Shepard," Hanrahan called through the door. "This is Bill Hanrahan. What the hell are you doing?"

Shepard didn't answer.

"Bernie," came Lieberman's voice. "It's Abe Lieberman. You want to talk?"

The answer was silence.

"Shepard," tried Hanrahan. "You might want to think about ending it now and easy. I'd give it half an hour, forty-five minutes tops before things get really bad."

Shepard didn't answer.

"You think he hears us?"

"He hears us," said Lieberman.

Shepard moved from the door and went to the edge of the roof. Below him he could see a policeman in uniform leaning into his car. There were three police cars, one in front of the Shoreham Towers and two blocking the entrance to Fargo. There was no need to block the other end of the short street. It dead-ended at the rocks a few feet from the lake. There were about a dozen curious bystanders looking at the Shoreham, talking.

Shepard motioned the dog back, lifted the rifle, wrapping the strap around his left hand. Then he propped the weapon on the edge of the concrete parapet, aimed, and fired.

A streetlight shattered, hissed and went dead. The cop leaning into Shepard's car clambered inside. The few cops on the street went behind their cars. The bystanders, unsure of what to do, went running toward their houses or into the lobby. A few simply stood there, not understanding what had happened.

Then one of the cops shouted, "Find cover. Get off the street."

And a woman screamed, went into total panic, and had to be dragged into the doorway of an apartment building across the street.

Lights were going on in windows all along the block in front of and below Bernie Shepard. He aimed again and took out a second streetlight. And then a third. The street went silent as Shepard moved back inside his concrete bunker.

The passageway in front of the door to the roof was narrow, not enough room for Lieberman and Hanrahan to stand at the same level. The light was dim, a single bulb behind them at the foot of the stairs where a uniformed officer stood with a rifle.

Lieberman and Hanrahan had guns in their hands, but both men knew that if Bernie Shepard decided to open the door and use the same weapon he had used on his wife and Beeton, there would be very little left of them to identify.

"What now?" asked Hanrahan.

"We wait for Kearney," said Lieberman.

That was when they had heard the first shot.

"Shit," sighed Hanrahan. "Shit, shit . . ."

Then the second shot and the third.

The radio on the hip of the officer with the rifle sputtered, and a less-than-calm voice crackled, "Sniper fire. I think it's from the roof. Shooting out streetlights."

"Sergeant," the officer at the foot of the stairs called.

"We heard," said Lieberman, touching Hanrahan's arm and indicating that they should go back down the stairs. When they reached the bottom, Lieberman told the officer to stay low and start shooting if the door above him began to open.

The officer nodded and got on his stomach, propping the rifle on the stairs. He knew what he was doing, and that made Lieberman feel a little, just a little, better.

The radio on the officer's hip crackled again and a voice both Lieberman and Hanrahan recognized came on.

"Lieberman," said Shepard.

Lieberman leaned over, unclipped the radio from the policeman's belt, and stood up, pressing the SEND button.

"I'm here, Bernie."

"I've planted enough explosives up here to take out this building and maybe half the block or more. You read?"

"I read."

"You believe?"

"I'm a believer," said Lieberman.

"Good," said Shepard calmly. "Make believers out of the rest of them or we're going to have a second Fourth of July. I want 'Channel Four News' up here, the blonde, Janice Giles. Up here with a camera for an exclusive interview."

"He's crazy," said Hanrahan, looking up at the door.

"Do it," said Shepard.

"I'll pass the request on to Captain Kearney," said Lieberman.

"It's not a request," said Shepard. "I want Kearney up here one o'clock tomorrow morning. No sooner. No later."

"Or . . . ?"

"I've got food, water, supplies, weapons, and a lot of explosives," he said.

"You're ready to die?" asked Lieberman.

"I'm ready."

"You want to talk? I'm up. I've had a coffee and a danish. The day is young."

"Come up alone," Shepard said. "No weapons."

Something—it may have been a laugh—crackled on the phone and then Shepard clicked off.

Lieberman handed his partner his jacket and gun and started back up the stairs.

"Abe, there's no point in going up there. He could blow your head off and throw you down for bait," said Hanrahan.

"I appreciate your support and confidence," Lieberman said over his shoulder.

He was at the top of the narrow stairwell now, and he knocked at the metal door. A scraping of metal on the other side, the flop and clang of metal against the roof, and the door opened slightly, the barrel of a shotgun inching out through the crack.

"Clean and alone," said Shepard.

"Clean and alone," said Lieberman, stepping onto the roof.

His first impression was that it was a different world,

cool, isolated. The sky was black with bright lights and a huge moon.

Shepard kicked the door shut and put his back against it, his shotgun leveled at Lieberman's stomach.

"Lift the pants legs, one at a time, as high as they'll go."

"I don't carry a drop, Bernie," Lieberman said, pulling up his pants legs one at a time.

"You're a man of your word, Lieberman, but words don't mean much tonight. Shirt up."

Lieberman lifted his shirt and turned around to show he was clean.

"Drop the pants."

"It's not a pretty sight," said Lieberman.

"I think I've seen worse," said Shepard.

In the darkness behind the concrete block barricade under the water tower, a dog growled sullenly.

"Satisfied?" asked Lieberman, pulling his pants up and fastening his belt.

"It's going to take a lot to satisfy me," he said.

Shepard looked calm, which might be a good or bad sign.

"You look like you're planning a long night," said Lieberman, nodding at the barricade.

"And a long day," said Shepard. "We can kick it around awhile Lieberman, but this is no shitcan. Your perp is standing in front of you confessing. Now, are you going to insult me by trying to talk me down?"

"Depends on what I risk by trying. It's nice up here."

Shepard looked around and at the moon.

"Peaceful at night," he said.

"You're going to get more people killed, Bernie. That what you want?"

"What I want I'll tell you. Now, I want you to look around. See the yellow circle on the water tower?"

Lieberman looked up at the water tower.

"Yes."

"I'm going to stay where I can see it," explained Shepard. "A shot from anything, handgun, shotgun, anything that hits that yellow spot will light us up all the way to the Michigan shore and turn this neighborhood into a people's rubble park."

Shepard had lowered the shotgun slightly so that it was no longer aimed at Lieberman, but both men knew how quickly it could come up and how much damage it could cause.

"I told you I believe you."

"But I want you to make them believe."

"I'll tell them."

"Now, you've got five minutes to say what you want to say," said Shepard, looking at his watch.

"You've got a case," said Lieberman. "You come home unexpectedly, wife's in bed with a fellow cop. Maybe he goes for his weapon. You—"

"You believe that?" asked Shepard.

"No."

"You think a jury will believe it?"

Lieberman looked at the setup under the water tower.

"No."

"Why don't you suggest we go for temporary insanity? Cop driven over the edge by the knowledge that his wife is cheating on him."

"Might go over," said Lieberman.

"It's not the truth, Abe."

"Maybe it is and you don't know it, Bernard."

"I don't want an out. I don't want to walk out of here in cuffs. I want Channel Four up here in the morning. It's getting late. Think it's time for you to go."

Shepard moved from the door, raised his shotgun again, and said, "You pull the bar away, open it, and go down."

"We've got to stop you, Bernie," said Lieberman, doing what he was told.

"You've got to try," Shepard countered.

Lieberman got the bar off and opened the metal door. It wasn't easy. Below him he could see Bill Hanrahan and the sniper. He took a step down and the door clattered shut behind him.

"What the hell is going on here?" Hanrahan called up the stairwell as Lieberman came down.

An answer suggested itself to Lieberman, but it wasn't time, nowhere near time, to let it out. He took his jacket and weapon back from his partner and went through the door leading back to the elevator.

The situation was bad, but by the time Hanrahan and Lieberman hit the street, it was much worse. Kearney had parked a block south and come through a backyard and an alley. He had heard the report of sniper fire from the roof.

Lieberman and Hanrahan were just coming through the front door of the Shoreham when Kearney stepped in front of them.

"I want the area clear for at least three blocks in all directions, right up to the lake. And find someplace for a command post, someplace where we can see the street and the front of this building. You talked to him?"

"I talked to him," said Lieberman.

They went into the lobby of the Shoreham. Residents, afraid to stay in their apartments, were gathered in small groups, arguing, listening, complaining, looking frightened. Lieberman led the way through the crowd to the laundry room. Hanrahan closed the door behind them.

Five minutes later Kearney knew what they knew, and the three policemen went carefully back to the front of the Shoreham. An ambulance had pulled up to the front of the hotel. Its lights were flashing.

Hanrahan grabbed a uniformed cop and started to give him orders to clear the area.

"How well you know Bernie Shepard?" Kearney asked Lieberman.

"Not well but long," said Lieberman, watching as a large dark car pulled up to the end of the street and was stopped by the police.

"He's good," said Kearney. "Picked the high ground. He can shut down Sheridan Road at rush hour."

"If it goes that long," said Lieberman.

"It'll go that long," said Kearney. "It'll go till he gets whatever he wants or blows up a good part of this city."

"You know what he wants, Captain?" asked Lieberman.

Kearney rubbed his broken nose and shrugged, but the shrug was a lie.

"No," he said. "What do you think he wants?"

"Someone else dead," said Lieberman.

The doors of the dark car were open and two men were being escorted toward the front of the Shoreham. The men were ducking and weaving. When they got close enough, Lieberman could see that one of them was a hastily dressed Marvin Hartz, chief of police, his hair disheveled, anger in his eyes. Hartz's gray suit and dark tie didn't match.

Hartz had fifteen years experience as liaison to the board of education. He had been a forgotten man till he took a chance, bolted the party, quit his job and came out strongly for Aaron Jameson, the black challenger for mayor. Hartz hadn't risked much. His wife had just died and the insurance and his pension would have left him warm and comfortable in Santa Fe. But Jameson had won and Hartz was chief of police. The man running behind Hartz was Captain Alton Brooks, SWAT director, in full uniform.

The chief was burly and big with a slightly stooped right shoulder. Brooks, compact, his face the gnarled color of stained oak, was known to his men as the Indian. To the rest of the Chicago Police Department who knew him, Brooks was the Cowboy.

Before Kearney could speak, Hartz said, "That's Shepard up there? Bernie Shepard just blew his wife and a cop away and climbed on the roof? What the hell for, for God's sake?"

Hartz looked up into the darkness as if it might yield some answer.

"Sergeant Lieberman talked to him a few minutes ago," said Kearney.

Hartz looked at Lieberman, trying to recognize him, a slight look of distaste on his lips.

"What does he want?" asked Hartz.

The word was that Hartz was anti-Semitic. Lieberman believed the word.

"Wants a Channel Four interview and to see Captain Kearney tomorrow morning at one."

"In the morning?" asked Hartz as if the requested hour were a confirmation of Shepard's madness.

"He's out of his mind," said Hartz, looking at Alton Brooks for support.

Brooks blinked once.

Lieberman wanted Kearney to take over, but Kearney had turned to watch the medics removing Andy Beeton and Olivia Shepard in body bags.

"He may be out of his mind, but he's not stupid," said Lieberman. "He says the roof is rigged with explosives. He says he has an arsenal up there."

"He's bluffing," said Hartz.

"I don't think so," said Lieberman.

"Shepard doesn't bluff," added Alan Kearney. "If he says it's rigged, it's rigged."

"I'm not convinced," said Hartz. "Kearney, what the fuck is he doing? What does he want with you?"

Kearney watched the door of the ambulance close.

"I don't know."

"Well," bellowed Hartz. "I'll tell you what he's getting. Shit. That's what he's getting. I want him down and I don't care how. Down and fast. The mayor'll be getting up in an hour or two, and he'll be on my ass about this. If Shepard isn't down by then, I'll be on your ass."

"He's picked a good spot," said Brooks, looking around the street. "High ground. What about doors to the roof?"

"One door," said Lieberman. "Steel. He's got it blocked and locked. The stairway is narrow."

"Copter or blow open the door," said Brooks.

"And Bernie Shepard pulls the plug on the whole neighborhood," said Kearney.

"Look . . ." Hartz began, having no idea what he wanted anyone to look at. Brooks decided to save him.

"I don't think he's got the roof wired. If he does, we can spot it from the copter and back away."

"And if he does have it rigged?" asked Kearney.

"Then," said Hartz, "we have a goddamn circus. Who the hell does he think he is—God?"

Hartz was looking at Lieberman now, so Lieberman answered, "Something like that."

Hartz shook his head and checked his watch.

"The hell with it. Brooks, get a copter up there."

"I'll need light to look for wires. Sun'll be up in an hour."

"May not have wires," said Lieberman. "Could all be plastic explosives."

"You were up there," said Hartz. "Did you see wires, anything that would prove any of this claim?"

"I saw Shepard. That convinced me."

"All right. All right," said Hartz holding up his hands as if he were calling for all present to be calm, which Lieberman found amusing since only Hartz seemed to be on the verge of losing control.

"First light comes, you send someone up there in a copter. Take him out, gas him out. Get him before he talks to any television people. Before the mayor gets up. Why the hell does he want to talk to goddamn television?"

"I don't know," said Kearney.

"Okay. Why does he want to talk to you?"

"Don't know," said Kearney.

"I'll take a look at that door," said Brooks, moving into the lobby. Hartz started after him into the building, changed his mind, and took a few steps in the direction of his waiting car before he stopped, turned to Kearney and Lieberman, and pointed at them.

"I want him down."

With that as an exit line, the chief of police went back to his car, being careful to walk as close to the protection of the building as possible.

"You want a coffee, Captain?" Lieberman asked.

Kearney shook his head no.

"What's the longest you ever stayed awake?" asked Lieberman.

Kearney looked at him.

"Two days, two nights on a stakeout," he answered.

"Lots of coffee."

"Lots of coffee. You don't think Brooks will get him down?"

"No," said Lieberman. "You?"

"No," said Kearney. "Not Bernie Shepard. I'll have the coffee, Sergeant."

In his fourth-floor apartment across the street from the Shoreham where he lived alone, Jason Belding, DDS, a portly man in his early forties, stood fully dressed sipping his tea and looking out of his living room window.

His lights were out and his television on with the first uninformative reports about what was taking place across the street. Gunfire, reports of a double murder, the possibility of a police officer being involved. That was it.

Jason watched the police hugging the building, watched the ambulance pull away, watched his neighbors' faces in their windows, watched the first television news truck pull up at the end of the street where the police stopped it.

Jason Belding had a perfect view. He considered calling in and canceling his morning appointments, but he quickly abandoned the idea. It wasn't the loss of money. That was no problem. People were counting on him. He had a successful pedodontics practice with offices both downtown in Chicago and in the Laurel Plaza Office Center in Wilmette, and he had never missed a day of work in his life.

The doorbell rang.

Jason was not surprised. It was early, but the Traneks or Hurlbets would be up and frightened. They would, when they thought it was a reasonable hour, knock at his door, ask him, as the only professional in the building, what was going on. They would seek his advice and comfort and Dr. Jason Belding, who had spent the last twelve years of his life tricking children into opening their reluctant mouths, would reassure them.

Belding walked across the recently cleaned white carpet and opened the door. The man in front of him was big. Jason considered slamming the door, but the man was holding his wallet open and showing a large silver badge.

"Police," said Hanrahan.

"What can I do for you, Officer?"

Hanrahan stepped past the dentist and into the apartment. Jason Belding had to balance and juggle to keep from spilling his tea.

"You can go on vacation for a few days," said Hanrahan looking around and moving to the window.

The place was too neat and tidy to suit him, but it would do.

"I don't . . . ," Belding began.

"Under City Ordinance 234 the city of Chicago Police Department is commandeering your apartment for the duration of this emergency."

Hanrahan stepped back in front of the confused Belding.

"You will be compensated for your inconvenience. Lives are at stake and your cooperation will be appreciated. You will be sent a letter of thanks from the mayor. Just pack a couple of things and call us tomorrow."

Belding reached over to the still-open door to close it, but a pair of uniformed police carrying equipment and a large bag from Wendy's brushed past him.

"I'm a dentist," Belding called to Hanrahan, who stood looking out the window.

"That's okay," said Hanrahan as the police began to set up equipment. "I had all mine pulled two years ago. Harris, when you get that set up, will you help the good doctor pack his things?"

The first light of sun shimmered far out on Lake Michigan. Lieberman stood watching from his car parked at the end of the street a block north of Fargo. It was early, but Bess was probably up and he had no idea when he'd get another chance to call. He pulled out his cellular phone and dialed home. If she didn't answer on the second ring, he would hang up and try again later.

Bess answered before the second ring.

"Hello."

"It's me."

"You're all right?"

"Of course I'm all right," he said. "Don't I sound all right?"

"You could be pretending. Wait, I'm not awake. What time is it?"

"Almost five," he said. "I got a call. You remember Bernie Shepard?"

"Bernie . . ."

"We went to his wedding four, five years ago."

"I remember."

"He shot his wife and another cop."

"I appreciate your waking me up to tell me."

"I'm sorry," Lieberman said, "but I don't know when I'll be home. Shepard's got himself barricaded on his apartment roof."

Somewhere in the distance from the south, toward downtown, Lieberman thought he heard a humming sound.

"Thank God he's not Jewish," sighed Bess.

"What?"

"I'm sorry," she said. "I'm still waking up. Did you make coffee? No, the kids. It's just if he were Jewish, the newspapers, the . . . You know what I mean."

"I know," said Lieberman.

The humming was definite now and coming closer.

"Will I see you for dinner?"

"I'll try."

"I've got a building committee meeting tonight. We'll have to eat early."

Bess had recently been elected president of Temple Mir Shavot, a position Abraham Lieberman had adroitly avoided. With the temple about to move into the newly renovated facility that had recently been the Fourth Federal

Bank of Skokie on Dempster Street, Bess was almost always at a meeting.

"If I can be home, I'll be home. If I can be home early, I'll be home early."

He had seldom talked to Bess about his work, but he had an urge, almost a need, to tell her about his dream, about Frankie Kraylaw.

"Bess, you remember . . ."

"What's that noise?" she asked.

Lieberman looked up.

"A helicopter."

Bernie Shepard sat, his back against the sleeping bag, his rifle on his lap, his eyes closed. The dog looked up toward the lake.

"I hear it," said Shepard without opening his eyes.

Slowly, crouching low, Shepard turned and leveled his rifle toward the rising sun, propping it on the top of his concrete-block barrier. The helicopter moved toward him slowly as Shepard turned on his radio and adjusted it till he could hear a voice from the helicopter saying, "No sign of him. Looks as if he's behind some concrete blocks under the water tower. No sign of any explosives, but they could be behind the blocks. We're moving in for a good look and a clean shot. When we've got him pinned down, we'll move in and launch the gas. If we can get close enough, I'll put it behind those blocks."

Shepard raised his rifle, looked through the sight, and fired. The shot smashed through the window of the copter. Almost immediately return fire shot out of the open door of the copter.

"Fire from the roof," came the voice from the helicopter. "Am returning fire and moving . . ."

Before the pilot could finish, Shepard fired again.

"Can't get any closer," came the voice on the radio. "We're launching now."

A gas grenade soared out of the open door of the helicopter, hit the roof a few yards from the concrete barricade, and rolled forward. Shepard fired again as the copter rose suddenly.

As it rose, Shepard leaped over the barricade, grabbed the grenade and threw it over the side of the building.

Inside the apartment of Jason Belding, DDS, Chief of Police Hartz, Alton Brooks, and Alan Kearney stood at the window, watching the helicopter and listening to the radio Brooks held in his hand.

"Son of a . . . We're getting out of here before he gets lucky and hits us."

"If he wanted to hit them, he would have hit them," said Kearney.

Brooks turned to the chief.

"I can tell them to make another run."

"And maybe lose two men and a million-dollar helicopter," sighed Hartz. "Turn that off."

Brooks switched off the radio.

"We knew he had a radio," said Hartz, turning from the window. "Radio silence . . ."

"He could hear the copter two miles away," said Brooks. "The man's not deaf."

Hartz's face was red. He turned, punched one of Dr. Jason Belding's best tables with his fist, and looked at Kearney as if he were somehow responsible for the situation.

"I've got to see the mayor in less than an hour and give him a report on this. Kearney, this operation is yours. Get him off that damned roof."

Hartz motioned to Brooks to join him and moved across the room. They almost collided with Lieberman as they went out and closed the door.

Through the window, Kearney watched as Hartz and Brooks carefully made their way to the side of the building and disappeared toward the back.

"Everybody cleared out of the building yet?" Kearney said, turning to Lieberman.

"They're running a double check now. Want some food?"

"Coffee."

Lieberman went into the kitchen. Coffee was brewing. He found cups on a shelf, poured two, and went back into the living room, handing one to Kearney, who took it with a nod of thanks.

"Traffic's diverted off Sheridan both ways to Clark. We're issuing warnings to the media suggesting that if anyone can see the tower, Shepard can see them and probably reach them with that rifle."

"What can he see from up there, Sergeant?"

"A hell of a lot, Captain. A hell of a lot."

"He can shut down half of East Rogers Park," said Kearney.

"There are those who might think that a humanitarian act."

Kearney drank his coffee and continued to look out the window.

"I've heard about your sense of humor, Lieberman," he said. "This isn't the time for it."

"It comes unbidden," said Lieberman. "Genetic. Part of the burden of my people. Can I ask you something?"

"Go ahead."

"You know what he's going to tell Channel Four?"

"I think so."

"And?"

"If we don't get him down soon, it's going to be a long twenty-four hours."

Frankie Kraylaw looked up at the television set at the end of the counter of the Speed King Donut Shop. He had been stopping at the Speed King on Devon for the past few months. Before that he had gone to the Mister Donut on Broadway, but Frankie and one of the other regulars, a bread truck driver named Bratkovic, had exchanged words. Frankie, teeth gleaming, little-boy smile on his face, hair over his eye, had sidled up to Bratkovic, a quiet corner smoker who liked to read the paper in peace before he made his rounds.

"Notice you in here every morning," Frankie had said.

Bratkovic had grunted.

"You know," Frankie had said, looking around at the four other predawn customers, who ignored him. "Christ died for your sins."

"Who asked him?" Bratkovic had answered.

"No one had to . . ."

But Bratkovic had cut him off with a call to the black woman in uniform serving coffee and sinkers.

"Elyse," he said, ignoring Frankie. "Move this guy and keep him away from me, or you'll be makin' a 911."

Elyse had sighed deeply, looking at her other early morning regulars for sympathy. Three ignored her or pretended to. Two others gave little smiles of sympathy.

"It's not that easy to deny the Lord," said Frankie.

Bratkovic looked up from his newspaper at Frankie, who was now about a foot from his face.

"Get out of my face."

Bratkovic had shoved Frankie as Elyse leaned over the counter saying, "Now, listen, young . . ."

But the push ended the peace and promise of salvation.

Frankie stood up, grabbed the glass sugar dispenser, and swung it at Bratkovic's face. Elyse's hand had reached over in time to keep the dispenser from hitting the bread truck driver in the face. But it had caught him in the ear.

Customers were backing out of their booths and off the stools. Coffee spilled. Bratkovic's ear was bleeding, and since the top of the sugar dispenser had come off, the blood was mixed with white glistening flecks.

It took two customers and Elyse to pull Bratkovic off Frankie, who wouldn't stop smiling.

"No fuckin' safe place to have a cup of coffee," Bratkovic screamed. "You crazy sons of bitches are coming out of the toilets."

Frankie, his nose now bloody, just smiled as he wished he had something sharp and heavy he could plunge into the eye of the blasphemer, lying on his belly.

That was two months ago. He had now become a regular

at the Speed King Donut Shop and had selected another regular, an old woman who always wore a black hat, who looked as if she might be in great need of salvation.

He was considering approaching her when the man on the television began talking about a policeman on a roof who had killed his wife and someone else.

All thoughts of the salvation of old women in black hats fled.

The man on the television speculated, said early reports were that the policeman had found his wife in bed with another man.

"Then," said Frankie softly to himself, "he was but the arm of the Lord and will be taken unto his breast."

"Huh?" asked the man behind the counter.

"More coffee," said Frankie.

The family, yes, he thought. The family is the only salvation for civilization. The husband must hold the family together. It is God's way. Always was. His own father had held his family together with a strong hand and a mighty heart.

Frankie Kraylaw loved his wife, loved his little boy, loved the Lord and the memory of his own mother and father. But the Lord knew best and the Lord had told Abraham to get rid of his wives and sacrifice his son, Isaac.

"If you do not put your faith in the Lord and let him guide your thoughts and your hand, that is an abomination."

"You talking to yourself or me?" asked the counterman, who was beginning to think that this kid with the goofy smile was losing him some of the early morning regulars.

"Sorry," said Frankie, getting up.

"Don't act so nuts," the counterman said, leaning over. "My advice. You can control it, control it. If not, keep it home or take it someplace else."

"I understand," said Frankie, looking over at the old woman in the black hat.

He did not want to lose her. God had put her salvation in his hands. The man with the mint breath behind the counter should have his eyes plucked out, for he had no use for them. He was blind to the truth and the ways of the Lord.

Frankie smiled and walked to the door of the doughnut shop, and the counterman dreaded the thought that the kid with the goofy smile would probably be back the next day.

The living room of the sixth-floor apartment of the Shoreham Towers was a beer-bottle, ash-strewn mess. Officer Sandra Anxman opened the door with a passkey and stepped in with Officer Craig Pettigrew behind her, carrying a clipboard.

"And," said Anxman, "he's all the time telling me it doesn't count as overtime, when the union contract says . . ."

The look and smell of the apartment hit her, and Anxman said, "Who the hell lives here—Porky Pig?"

"Binyon, Carl, and McAulife, David," said Pettigrew, checking his clipboard.

Pettigrew put the clipboard under his arm, and the two officers began to check the apartment, looking behind sofas, opening closets.

"You'd think," Anxman said, pushing open the bedroom door, "in a building like this . . . Look at this crap. Shepard shot the wrong fuckin' tenants. He would have done the health department a favor by painting the walls with the guys who live here."

"I'm not touching anything," said Pettigrew. "Smells like shit in here. Let's go."

"Check it off," Anxman agreed. "No one here."

Anxman stepped out and Pettigrew took one last look at the apartment, shook his head, and said, "How do people live like this?"

Before the door was completely closed, Anxman was saying, "So I'm calling it overtime. I don't give a shit what Walsh calls it. He can talk to the union."

When the voices of the two police officers had faded, a closet door in the apartment opened and Carl and Dave crawled out from beneath a pile of ratty blankets.

"Did you hear? Porky Pig? Christ, we did a search like that in Kuwait City, we'd be dead meat. Stupid-ass cops."

Carl stood. He was no more than thirty, but life had not treated him well. Actually, life had treated him as he had treated it. His hair was naturally light and curly, which saved him from the impossible task of combing it. He liked to think that he looked a little like Chuck Norris, which wasn't the least bit true. Dave crawled out after him, a thin creature with a military haircut and no shirt. Dave had a single tattoo on his chest, an ice-cream bar with one bite missing. Dave began searching the rubble for something while Carl went on, "You think this room is a mess?"

"I can't find my shoes, Carl."

Carl, brooding, cleared a space for himself on a chair and plopped down.

"That's not the fuckin' issue here, Dave. The issue here is sanitary conditions. You like the cops sayin' you're unsanitary is what I'm asking you?"

Dave pushed a pile of newspapers out of the way and realized by the pregnant pause that he was expected to supply some answer.

"I suppose I don't like it much."

"Like what?" Carl said.

"Whatever we're talking about I'm not supposed to like. I'm looking for my shoes here, Carl. Give me a break."

Dave stepped over a filthy pillow on the floor and saw his shoe.

"No one kicks us out of the place we pay rent for," said Carl, hitting the arm of the sofa with the flat of his hand. "We've got our self-respect."

Dave had one more shoe to find. Instead of the shoe, he turned up an unopened can of Miller beer.

"This," he said, "should be in the refrigerator. God. I do not like being barefoot. Makes me feel . . ."

". . . vulnerable," Carl supplied. "That's what I was talking about, Dave. Your self-respect."

Dave had heard it before.

41

"I know. I know. We get our jobs back. We get our self-respect."

"I don't like hiding in closets, Dave. I tell you that for a fact. It doesn't become a man to hide in closets. We had enough hiding in that fuckin' desert. From now on . . ."

"We hide from no man," Dave completed, finding his second shoe. "Hot damn."

Dave displayed the shoe proudly, but Carl paid no attention.

"I'm getting an idea here, Dave," Carl said, sitting up.

Carl looked up at the ceiling and Dave looked at Carl, not liking what he saw in his friend's face.

"Don't upset me, Carl. I just want to get my shoes on and . . ."

"When's the last time we cleaned the rifles?" asked Carl, and Dave knew he was in some deep, deep shit.

4

Alan Kearney checked the clock on the dashboard of his car, opened the door of his glove compartment, and took out his electric razor. It was a minute or two before seven. He had come out of the apartment to be alone, have a cup of coffee, and try to think.

Behind him, at the far end of the street, the yellow-and-black wooden barriers were in place with two police cars behind them and a quartet of men and women in uniform keeping the curious out. The Shoreham apartments and all the apartments and houses on Fargo had been evacuated, the residents being promised motel money and a per diem that, Kearney knew, would be damned hard for them to collect.

He shaved, losing himself in the hum and the task, sorry when he had finished. He found a place he had missed under the chin, another near his right ear. He stroked them slowly, turned off the razor, and checked his cheek with his palm.

He had a spare shirt, a change of underwear, and a tooth-brush in the trunk, emergency supplies. He would get to them later. Kearney got out of the car with his plastic foam cup of no-longer-hot coffee and walked toward the lake. The sky was clear and the September sun hot. An hour earlier Kearney had checked with the weather bureau. There was no reasonable possibility of rain. Kearney would have bet that Shepard had checked with the weather bureau before deciding that last night was the night to kill his wife and her lover.

He wandered out onto the beach, stopped near an overflowing garbage can, finished his coffee, and threw his crumpled cup atop the heap.

He had put it off long enough. Kearney walked back to his car, looking up at the empty windows, sensing the vacant apartments, wondering if there were cats and dogs who would, if this thing went on, howl inside with fright and hunger.

Kearney opened his car door, reached for his radio, pushed the button, and said, "Bernie, are you monitoring?"

There was a long pause and Shepard answered. "I hear you."

"How about letting me up there now?" asked Kearney. "It's been a long night for both of us."

"And we're looking at a longer day," answered Shepard.

"Bernie . . ."

"Not now. Not on the radio. You sweat it out. I'll give you one change. Make it an hour earlier, midnight. You come up here at midnight. That's a time people will remember. Midnight."

"Why, Bernie?"

"You know why," Shepard said evenly. "And when I'm finished with you, everyone in the city'll know why. By the time you come up here tonight, you'll be like me. No reputation, no future, nothing. I'm making that a ten-four and out."

There was a click, a shimmer of static, and nothing. Kearney shook his head. And then the radio came to life again and Hanrahan's voice said, "Channel Four's truck is here."

Kearney looked back down the street at the white van. He couldn't see it, but he knew there was a lightning streak on the side and a big yellow 4.

"I see it. I'm on the way."

Before heading back down the street, Kearney opened the trunk of his car, removed his clean shirt and tie, and tried not to wonder what the day would be like.

* * *

Bernie Shepard needed rest. He closed his eyes, willing himself to remain alert, not quite fall asleep.

And he remembered when his eyes were closed that he had once had a brother and a dog and a mother and father. And he remembered that by the time he was eighteen, all of them were dead.

Bernie's parents, Lorna and Harold, ran a cleaning store and laundry service on Twenty-second Street not far from Farragut High. Did a decent business in neighborhood trade and had a contract with the high school for uniforms. Harold, who had come over from Cardiff to escape the mines, considered himself a success and was considered a success by those in the Old Country. He had married a Scots girl his first year in the States. He had no dreams of an empire. A good house, three hearty meals, a safe wife, and sons who obeyed were the extent of his ambitions. And then the neighborhood began to change. Back in Cardiff neighborhoods did not change.

When the neighborhood started to go black and Hispanic, business actually got better, but living conditions for Bernie and his brother, Don, got worse.

Donnie was the big brother, at least the older brother by three years. They were both about the same size and when they could, outside of school and in, they traveled together with their dog. Harold told them, taught them by raised voice and example to take no "crap or folly" from any man. And so people knew the Shepard brothers, learned not to mess with them and the alley dog who acted a little crazy.

The brothers had purposely given the dog no name. They had seen *Hondo*. John Wayne's dog had no name in that one. And *The Rainmaker*. Wendell Corey's dog didn't have a name either. There was something a little scary about a dog who had no name, a dog who had nothing to lose.

The Shepard boys and their dog were tested just enough to prove they were not just putting on an act. Don spent four months in Juvenile for almost killing a black kid. The dog was shot by a policeman when it was trapped in an alley behind a grocery store on Ogden Avenue after tearing off the ear of a crazy named Ollie who tried to kick shit out of Bernie.

They never got another dog. That was when the Shepards decided to move north. It was the first move north. There were other moves later until they were at the very northwest corner of the city, and Harold Shepard, a somewhat dull-witted—even to his children—bull of a man vowed that they would move no more, that he would build a stone wall around his house and arm himself and his boys before he would move again.

Shepard's parents died in an automobile crash on Higgins Road in 1960 when Bernie was seventeen and Donnie was just getting out of jail. They sold the house and lived together in North Uptown. Bernie drove a drop-off truck for the *Chicago Tribune*. Donnie tried car sales and found he didn't have the knack for getting people to trust him.

Donnie found other ways to make money and even a way to lose his life. Bernie watched his brother's decline, watched his friends, watched his drug habit, knew and didn't want to know.

And then one day a cop was at his door, a cop with a bored pockmarked face, wearing a sweaty suit. The cop told him that Donnie was dead. The cop, whose name was Dickerson, could have simply said, "I'm sorry," and walked away, but he didn't. He came in, talked patiently to the angry young man, invited him to his house for dinner and talk.

Bernie had said no, but he went. Dickerson lived alone, had never married, was a great cook and a decent housekeeper. Once, when he had first gone to see Dickerson, he had thought the cop was queer, but he was wrong. Dickerson had two women, both ugly, as ugly as he was. Either one would have married him. He would have none of it.

"Not built for it, kid," he told Bernie. "Some are. Some aren't. You? I'd say you're not, but it's worth a try."

And Bernie had, with Dickerson's help, become a cop.

And without Dickerson's help he had decided, before he was even twenty, that he wanted a wife, a family, another dog. He wanted a perfect family, in the image of the one that had been taken from him.

He saw the filth of the city, the people who destroyed each other and the innocent, and Shepard decided that he would build his own world; and when he was forty-seven years old he decided that the world would begin with the girl named Olivia who had been introduced to him by his partner, Alan Kearney, his partner, who reminded him of his brother, Donnie.

"Nova's good, huh?" asked Maish, his somber bulldog face turned toward his brother. Maish was the overweight, white-aproned judge and jury of Maish's T&L Deli on Devon. He had presided over the T&L for more than twenty of his sixty-six years. Before that, he had a place on Roosevelt Road, kept it till he was the last white in the neighborhood and it wasn't safe anymore.

"Nova's good," agreed Lieberman, digging into his lox, onion, and cream cheese omelette and guiding it down with a toasted onion bagel.

Kearney had told Lieberman to take two or three hours off, get some rest, and keep in touch. Lisa and the kids would be up now, getting ready for work and school. Bess might or might not be up. Abe Lieberman did not want to walk into the confusion of his grandchildren's requests or the paradoxes of his daughter. He would wait it out till they had left. He loved them, but he was beyond tired.

"So what is it this time?" asked Maish, pouring his brother a cup of coffee.

The place was empty except for Abe and the three women, Melody Rosen, Herschel's daughter, who clerked at Bass's Children's Shop down the street and always stopped for a toasted bagel and coffee; Gert Bloombach, a sack of a woman who worked in a law office downtown and came to the T&L every Tuesday and Thursday morning for a lox omelette and a cup of tea; and Sylvie Chen, Howie's daughter, a nice-looking girl with thick glasses who never ordered the same thing twice.

Early mornings at the T&L belonged to the working women and the cops Lieberman had introduced to the place. The Alter Cockers, all of them retired, on pensions, between jobs, started to drift in around ten.

"Cop named Shepard killed his wife and another cop," said Lieberman.

Maish nodded and refilled Sylvie Chen's cup. Sylvie was the only other customer at the counter. Both Gert and Melody were alone in booths.

"That one. Heard it on the radio on the way in," said Maish. "Shepard? He ever come in here? Sounds familiar?"

"Could be," said Lieberman, wondering whether he should go for another bagel.

Maish's face showed nothing. Maish's face never showed anything. Years ago Syd Levan had dubbed him Nothing-Bothers-Maish and it had stuck. Lieberman knew his brother enjoyed the nickname, had always wanted a nickname, and in high school had desperately tried to get friends and acquaintances to call him Studs, in honor of his favorite character.

"They gonna make .500?" asked Maish.

It was Lieberman's favorite subject, the Cubs.

"I look that bad you gotta cheer me up by talking baseball?"

"You look that bad," admitted Maish.

Each year Lieberman's goals for his Cubs changed by midseason. In a good year they were shooting for the pennant. In an average year they were shooting for .500. In a bad year they were shooting for individual goals. Maybe one hundred RBIs each for Dawson and Daniels. Maybe thirty-plus homers for Sandberg, Dawson, or Daniels, and a .300 year for Sandberg and Grace. Maybe a return of Sutcliffe, the hero of Lieberman's grandson Barry, to the Cubs. Four years ago Lieberman had taken Barry to a Cubs game. They had sat in a box right behind third base, courtesy of Andy Frain himself, the founder of the uniformed usher army, for whom Lieberman had done a favor or two. Sutcliffe had thrown Barry his warm-up ball and gone on to pitch a five-hit shutout.

Just remembering that day made Lieberman feel better.

"Yetta's all right?" asked Abe.

"Yetta's Yetta," answered Maish, nodding to Gert, who had nodded for her check. "She's got a leg now. It doesn't do what she tells it sometimes."

Maish made out Gert's check.

"Dr. Lerner?"

"Dr. Lerner," sighed Maish, ripping the check off the pad. "He says she's getting old. You expect willful limbs when you get old. That, he said, should be the worst of her problems."

"Reassuring," said Abe, pushing his plate away.

Maish brought the check to Gert, who fussed through her oversized purse and came up with a five-dollar bill. Maish brought it back behind the counter.

"She orders the same thing every day," he whispered to his brother. "Same price. She always asks for a check and always looks at it and always gives me a five-dollar bill so she can have change for the bus. Life's little ironies."

Abe gave his brother a five-dollar bill and got up. Abe always paid and Maish almost always gave him a bag of something "to take with for Bess, Lisa, the kids."

Today's bag, Lieberman could tell from the smell, was ruggalah.

"Sam working today?" he asked, moving to the door.

"Why not?" answered Maish.

Sam was Maish's only child. Sam was a producer at Channel 4.

"I think I'll maybe make a call and stop at the house."

Maish reached under the counter and came up with the house phone. Abe pulled his address book out of his pocket, found the number he was looking for, and hit the buttons for the Kraylaw apartment. The phone rang six times before Lieberman hung up.

"Bring the kids in for lunch if you get a chance Sunday."

"I will," said Abe, stepping out onto the sidewalk.

Most of the stores on this side of California Avenue were still closed. Leon's Fruits and Vegetables was open. Hempel's Bakery was open, but Hinkey's Bike Shop, the savings and loan, and everything else was sound asleep. Further east, toward Lake Michigan, past Western Avenue, Devon was alive. The immigrants rose early, even the Kung Fu Academy was open for skinny kids and dreaming adults who wanted a shot of self-esteem before work or school or walking the street.

Lieberman hit Birchwood a little after eight. Lisa's car was gone. In its place in front of the house stood a white Buick, a not-very-new white Buick. Lieberman considered continuing on, but if Todd's car was parked and he wasn't in it, Bess was inside with him. He parked and, armed with his sweet-smelling ruggalah, got out of his car and entered his house.

"Abe," shouted Bess when she heard the door open. "You've got company."

"You've got company," Lieberman repeated to himself. Not, We've got company. Bess was paving the way for total abandonment.

"I saw the car," said Lieberman, moving to the kitchen and looking at his wife and son-in-law seated at the table.

Bess was wearing her red-and-black suit, which meant serious business for someone. The silver necklace around her neck, the one he had bought for her when they went to Mérida, Mexico, on vacation four years ago, convinced Lieberman that she was not only serious but she expected to triumph.

Todd smiled up at him, a long-suffering smile. Todd Cresswell was a bit on the thin side, sandy of hair. He was wearing a dark sweater, navy slacks, a red tie, and a very pained expression which, Lieberman thought, made his smile look like the first pangs of constipation.

"I brought ruggalah," said Lieberman, placing the bag on the table.

"I'm glad you're here," said Bess, rising. "I've got to go.

Breakfast meeting at the synagogue. Irving Hamel is trying to convince us to get a bigger bank loan and drag the building renovation fund drive out for two years."

"And," said Lieberman, knowing for sure now that he was being abandoned, "you've got the votes? I can tell from the canary feathers coming out of your mouth."

"Ida Katzman and Rabbi Wass both," she said triumphantly.

"Rommel hasn't got a chance," said Lieberman, dipping into the bag for a ruggalah. It felt honey sweet and sticky.

Bess gave him a kiss on the cheek and patted Todd's shoulder. Todd gave his mother-in-law a suffering smile.

"Good-bye," she said.

"Good-bye," said Lieberman and his wife was gone.

He turned to his son-in-law.

"I dubbed Irving Hamel 'Rommel,' " Lieberman explained to avoid the inevitable. "He's a lawyer, young. He blitzkriegs."

Todd nodded.

"So," said Lieberman, settling in for the siege. "I've got about twenty minutes. I've been up all night and I need a shower and some rest. Have a ruggalah."

"That's all right," said Todd. "I've got a class at nine."

With that, Todd reached into the bag and pulled out one of the small honey pastries. He looked at it and said, " 'Darkness lies upon my eyes.' "

Lieberman's sigh was deep.

"Euripides," he said.

"That's right," Todd said, looking up with interest. "*Heracles*. How did you . . . ?"

"He's your favorite," said Lieberman. "Remember the ground rules, Todd. Don't quote Greek tragedies. I don't want to hear dead Greeks I don't understand. I'm a tired cop."

"I've tried, Abe," Todd said, looking at the refrigerator.

Lieberman resisted the urge to join him.

"Maybe you should try harder," said Lieberman.

"I want Lisa back. I want the kids back. I'm tired of

'Rockford Files' reruns on television. I've got to tell you this. I even tried to go out on a date, with a new instructor, from Yale."

"A woman?"

"Of course a woman," said Todd.

"I'm sorry," said Lieberman, resisting a new urge to fill his cheeks with ruggalah and make an insane face at his son-in-law.

"I don't even know what I did wrong. I don't even know what to do. I'm a domestic creature, Abe."

The phone rang.

"I'll talk to her again," Lieberman promised, moving to the phone.

" 'A man shall be commended according to his wisdom,' " said Todd. " 'But he that is of a perverse heart shall be despised.' "

"Todd . . . ," Lieberman began warningly.

"That's not Greek. It's the Old Testament. Proverbs twelve, verse eight. You don't want me to quote the Bible?"

"I don't want you to quote anything," said Lieberman. "God and Rabbi Wass forgive me. I'll talk to her."

Lieberman picked up the phone and said, "Lieberman."

"Nestor, Abe," Briggs said. "You are a popular man today. First, Bernie Shepard wants you on the case, now Hal Querez at the North says he needs you fast."

"He say why?" asked Lieberman, looking at Todd whose eyes searched his father-in-law's face for reassurance.

"I think it's El Perro," said Briggs. "But don't quote me on that. Hal wants you at the North fast."

"Call Bill Hanrahan. Tell him I had an emergency. I'll get there as fast as I can."

Lieberman hung up the phone and looked at Todd.

"You won't give up?" asked Todd.

Lieberman rose and motioned to Todd to get up too. Todd did so wearily.

"I don't sleep much," said Todd.

"I don't either," said Lieberman.

"I watch television most of the night," Todd confessed.

"Old movies, reruns of 'Andy of Mayberry,' anything to keep from being alone. And I eat, anything, everything. This will kill me, Abe."

Lieberman led his son-in-law out the kitchen and to the front door.

"It won't kill you, Todd. It may make you tired and fat, but it won't kill you."

"I trust you, Abe."

"I'm honored," said Abe, opening the front door.

"You're joking," said Todd. "I'm sincere."

"I'm sorry," said Abe. "People are murdering people and I've got to get an hour or two of sleep. I'll be my usual cheerful self tomorrow."

Todd started down the steps.

"Fill yourself with V-Eight," Lieberman said. "Few calories, some vitamins. Fills your stomach."

Todd stopped and looked back at him.

"That's your advice?"

"That and don't wear brown shoes with the navy slacks and sweater."

Lieberman closed the door and headed straight for the bedroom.

Cops owned houses. Even if they couldn't afford it, they owned houses. Even if the houses were two rooms and a crawl space, they owned. Success was owning a house. Owning a house was stability, a small piece of the American dream.

The house he parked in front of on Nordica just south of Foster, in the far northwest corner of the city a few miles from O'Hare airport, was brick, modest, and tiny. The lawn was neat and white concrete steps clean.

Hanrahan had done this before, at least forty times, once for another cop whose name he couldn't remember. That had been early in his drinking days. A double J&B and a pack of spearmint would carry him, but he knocked on this door with just the memory of the Molson beer from Shepard's refrigerator and the hint of a Velamint on his tongue.

She answered on the fourth knock and he knew that she knew.

"Mrs. Beeton?" he asked.

She was a big woman, blond, round pretty face, far too much makeup, looked around thirty. Her hair was short, brushed back. She was wearing a dark dress and a scared, defensive look that opened her eyes with the expectation of more horror.

"Yes," she said.

"My name's Hanrahan, Sergeant Hanrahan. Can I come in for a minute?"

She stepped back to let him enter and he entered, brushing against her, smelling a sweet perfume and fear. He moved to the right of the door and faced her.

"You want to close the door, Mrs. Beeton?"

The woman looked at the door, nodded, and pushed it closed.

"You know?" he asked.

"Andy," she said. "He's dead."

"Yes."

"It was on ... My mother heard it on the radio. She called. I got dressed. My mother is coming. She lives in Palos Heights. She should get here, if she doesn't hit too much traffic on the expressway, she should get here soon."

"Yes," said Hanrahan. "Can I do anything for you?"

"A policeman shot him?" she asked.

"Yes, Mrs. Beeton."

"Connie, my name is Connie. Before I married Andy my name was Connie Conroy."

"Irish," he said.

"No. Welsh. And Navaho," she said. "A policeman killed Andy?"

"Yes ma'am."

"Connie."

"Connie."

She moved past him into the living room and Hanrahan turned to face her.

"You want to sit? Want some . . . I've only got instant, but it's Taster's Choice."

"No, thank you."

The furniture in the room reminded Hanrahan of his own house. The chairs, sofa were old, comfortable. There was a large, colorful American Indian rug on the floor and the one huge painting on the wall was a scene of five or six Navaho Indians in the desert, shading their eyes with their hands, looking off the frame at something distant.

"I had my nails done yesterday," she said. "I'm sorry. I don't know why I said that."

"It's all right," said Hanrahan.

"I've got decaf," she said hopefully. "Would you mind staying till my mother gets here?"

"I'll stay," he said. "And a glass of ice water would be fine."

Though he had not been invited to sit, Hanrahan moved to a chair opposite Connie Beeton. He could see the Navahos on the wall from there.

"Why did the policeman . . . ?" she said, putting her hands flat on her knees, trying to remain calm.

"He—Sergeant Shepard—shot his wife too."

Connie Beeton made no move to get his water, which was fine with Hanrahan.

"I understand," she said. "You have any children, Officer . . . ?"

"Hanrahan, Sergeant. Two boys, both grown, a couple of grandchildren."

"We don't have any children," she said, smiling. "I work at the Eagle grocery, on Harlem."

She pointed over his shoulder in the direction of Harlem Avenue.

"I'm an assistant manager. We were planning to have a baby later this year," she said, patting her palms on her legs. "I forgot your water."

"Later," he said.

She nodded as if he had said something of great importance and then fell silent.

"He couldn't help it," she said finally, her eyes moist.

Hanrahan wasn't sure whether she was talking about Shepard or her husband.

"Yes," he said, now wanting that water.

"I knew he . . . I knew about the women," she said. "Andy stayed in shape. He went to college. Bachelor's degree in political science. I've got the degree on the wall in our room."

She started to rise.

"I believe you."

Connie Beeton sank back on the chair and looked at him.

"I think I'd like that water you offered," he said.

"I'm so sorry."

She leaped up and moved to the open door to the kitchen. He watched the Navahos and wondered what they were looking at as he heard the refrigerator door open and then the clunk of ice cubes.

"Mineral water," she said, hurrying back into the room.

"Thanks."

He took the glass and sipped; she went back to her chair and watched him as if his opinion of her water were of great importance.

The water was carbonated. Hanrahan hated carbonated water.

"Very good," he said with a smile.

"I loved him," she said. "Does it embarrass you for me to say that?"

"No," he said.

"He wasn't a bad man," she said.

"He was a fine police officer," said Hanrahan, forcing himself to take another drink.

A key scratched in the front door and Hanrahan stood up and faced it. The door opened and a woman about the same size and build as Connie entered the house. She looked at Hanrahan and then at Connie Beeton, who rushed to her arms.

Hanrahan looked into the eyes of the dark mother as she hugged her sobbing daughter, and he recognized her face.

He turned back to the painting of the Navahos on the desert and knew that he was right.

"I'll be going," he said.

The dark mother nodded and closed her eyes, and without knowing why he felt better than he had in a long time.

It was now officially labeled Operation Seven. The name had been chosen by Chief of Police Hartz after much thought and concentration. He had first considered giving the operation a color, Operation Red. No, red suggested blood. Blue, yellow? Certainly not yellow. Every color had a connotation. Names were no better. Operation Tower? Gave it too much importance. Operation Rogue? Shepard? Use the name of the street? Hartz settled on a number which, he hoped, had no meaning. Operation Seven.

The apartment of Jason Belding, DDS, which was now the operational command post of Operation Seven, had been transformed into an efficient, if somewhat messy, headquarters. "Somewhat messy" was a relative description. The furniture had been moved out of the way, used as convenient places to dump and pile. The kitchen was a place to stack half-finished cartons of coffee, Big Gulps of Coke, and Burger King bags.

At the moment, in what had a few hours ago been a living room, two men were checking their pampered portable television camera and sound equipment on the white living room carpet while Janice Giles memorized a list of questions in her notebook. Kevorkian had told her to get up there, get her questions asked, and get back downstairs on the remote. They had considered a live news break-in but decided against it. It would look too much like they were risking Janice's life. After the fact, when she was safe, that was a different story.

She could push it a little but not much. There just wasn't enough time if they were going to make the noon news. Kevorkian had also held out the possibility that the network might want to take the feed if it turned out to be good. Janice Giles intended to make it good.

When Alan Kearney came through the door, she moved toward him quickly.

"Captain Kearney," she said, holding out her hand.

"Miss Giles," Kearney said, taking it.

"Can we interview you on the street rather than in here before we go talk to Shepard?" she said.

Kearney released her hand and shook his head.

"You're giving me a choice," he said, walking past the cameraman and the sound man, who were up and ready. "I like that. You don't give me the option of saying no. Good bargaining technique. We use it a lot."

"Okay," Janice Giles said with her most winning you-caught-me smile, "will you talk to me on camera?"

"No," said Kearney, walking to the window and looking up at the tower.

"Chief Hartz . . ." she began.

". . . isn't here," said Kearney, still looking out of the window. "The man you're planning to talk to up there blew away his wife and a fellow officer a few hours ago. He has the gun he used and, we think, some weapons that can reduce you and your crew to a small rag and a spot of blood. You're here because Shepard wants to talk to you and we want to know what's on his mind."

Janice Giles, dressed in a green suit with a white silk blouse and costume pearl necklace, folded her arms and looked at Craddock, her cameraman, and Nowitz, the sound man. She indicated by her silent sigh that they all knew what was coming next. Craddock, a compact man in a blue short-sleeve pullover, was a year away from his thirtieth birthday. He thought he had seen it all. He closed his eyes to indicate to Janice that he too knew what was coming. Nowitz, however, had been at this for thirty years and didn't give a damn either way.

"And," said Janice Giles, "you want to look at the interview before we broadcast it. You want to censor the press."

Kearney started to speak, but she stopped him with a long-fingered hand.

"No, I take that back. You want to see the tape and then decide if you need to censor it."

"Through?" asked Kearney, trying to find a lopsided smile.

"For the moment," said Giles.

There was much about her that reminded Kearney of Carla Duvier. The thin model's figure with the perfect breasts, the pride. The way she looked at him, unblinking, determined, expecting to get her way, a blond daytime version of his dark fiancée.

Craddock and Nowitz had been through this before. Nowitz left his equipment on the rug and moved to the kitchen. Craddock plopped into a white chair, looking bored.

"You're not gonna get an issue here, Miss Giles," Kearney said. "No one is going to stop you or try to stop you from broadcasting whatever you damn please. If I tried, if Hartz tried, the mayor would rip our hearts out and make us clean up the blood."

"Colorful and graphic, but not original," said Giles, allowing just the touch of annoyance to curl her rather full lips into a near pout.

"You go up on that roof and you might come down in a bag," said Kearney. "That's not original either. You can point that out when they zip up your cameraman's body bag."

"I don't think Shepard wants to hurt me. I think he wants to use me," she said as Kearney took a step toward her.

"And you want to use him," said Kearney.

"Yes," she said. "That's my job."

"The people's right to know. They'll all be better-informed, responsible citizens if they have a little gore with their microwave dinners, right?"

Giles wanted to look at her watch but held back. She settled for a near whisper. "Wrong. I'm in the entertainment business. That man up there is worth ratings and a few minutes of entertainment. I didn't make it this way, but I can't say I don't enjoy my work. There are stories where I think I can do some good. Not many but a few. And not this one. Now I've got a question for you, Captain. Off the record. Are you a cop because you want to save the world?"

"You've got a point," said Kearney.

"Thanks."

"Okay," said Kearney. "You go up on the roof and you get your story, but we have one condition. Your sound man will be replaced by one of our men who Shepard doesn't know."

Nowitz, a sandwich of something in his hand, wandered back in from the kitchen and shouted, "No way. No fucking way."

"Forget it, Kearney," said Janice Giles.

The door to the apartment opened while Giles and Kearney looked at each other, Nowitz looked from one to the other, and Craddock looked as if he were falling asleep. Hanrahan stepped through the front door, read the scene, and stopped, waiting. Kearney shrugged.

"Then," he said, "we forget it."

"Chief Hartz . . . ," Janice Giles began.

"Miss Giles, it's his idea."

"It's bullshit," shouted Nowitz, putting the sandwich down on one of the embroidered white dining room chairs of Jason Belding, DDS.

"Let me get this straight," said Giles. "And for the record, Captain. You plan to have some cop go up on that roof pretending he's a sound man and then pull out a gun and shoot Officer Shepard."

"If the opportunity presents itself," said Kearney.

Giles looked at Craddock, whose eyes were completely closed, and then at Hanrahan, who seemed to be preoccupied with finding something in his teeth with his tongue. Nowitz, however, was properly incensed.

"Isn't that putting me and my cameraman in danger?" Janice Giles said. "Shepard could . . ."

"He could anyway," said Kearney. "Our man doesn't

shoot unless he has to. And if he does, you've got it all on tape for the news at noon. Take it or . . ."

"Your man won't know how to use our equipment," Giles said.

"He's a former movie technician," said Kearney. "Worked on a Chuck Norris and an Arnold Schwarzenegger movie."

"Wait a minute," Nowitz bleated, looking at Craddock for support. Craddock didn't even bother to shrug.

"He'll wait till I get my interview before he starts anything?" she asked, ignoring Nowitz.

Kearney nodded in agreement.

"Hold it. Hold it. Hold it," said Nowitz. "Giles, you dumb bitch. He's hanging you out. Who's gonna trust you after this? Your word won't be worth shit."

"Is this settled?" asked Craddock, opening his eyes and looking from Janice Giles to Alan Kearney.

"Ask the lady," said Kearney.

"It's settled," she said. And then she turned to Nowitz. "Norman, let's go in the other room and talk."

Nowitz moved to the kitchen door and kicked it open. Janice Giles followed him and Craddock went after them leaving Hanrahan and Kearney alone.

"You talked to Beeton's wife?"

"Yeah."

Kearney opened his mouth to say more, but the look on Hanrahan's face stopped him.

"Lieberman back?" Kearney asked.

"Querez wanted him at the North," said Hanrahan. "Some kind of gang business. Emergency."

"I'd call this an emergency, wouldn't you, Sergeant?" asked Kearney.

"Sergeant Lieberman'll get here as fast as he can," said Hanrahan.

Kearney looked back at the window.

"Hartz may just get that lady killed," said Hanrahan.

Kearney looked back at Hanrahan.

"Sergeant, between you and me, Chief Hartz . . . Forget it. Is Ballentine out there?"

"He's out there."

"You're sure Bernie never met him?"

"Ballentine says no. Just got on the force three weeks ago. Came from Houston," said Hanrahan looking at the kitchen door. There was a sizable footprint where Nowitz had kicked it. "He knows nothing about sound equipment. Doesn't even do home movies."

"It won't get that far," said Kearney.

"You're hoping, Captain."

"I'm praying, Sergeant."

"You think Ballentine has a shot in hell?"

"You got a way with words, Sergeant," said Kearney, knowing both he and Hanrahan thought Chief of Police Hartz was a major league asshole.

On the roof of the Shoreham Towers, Bernie Shepard took a drink from his canteen and poured some water into a cup for the dog. The dog drank carefully but noisily. When the knock came at the steel door, the cup was almost empty. The dog knocked it over with his nose and came up ready.

Shepard stood, cradled his shotgun, glanced around to be sure no helicopter was on the horizon, and moved to the door, the dog at his heels.

When the second knock came, Shepard called out, "Talk."

"Channel Four's here, Bernie," Abe Lieberman said. "Janice Giles, a cameraman, and a sound man."

Lieberman had made it back to the Shoreham just as Kearney was leading the crew into the lobby. He had pulled Kearney off to the side to tell him of a way they might want to consider for getting Bernie Shepard off the roof. Kearney said he would pass it on to Hartz. Then Lieberman had added, "I'm looking forward to a peaceful, happy retirement, spring in Scottsdale with the Cubs, winter in Georgia."

"I'm glad to hear that, Sergeant," Kearney had said impatiently.

"I'll risk it by giving some advice, Captain," said Lieberman. "I hear we've got a man going up there in place of one of the Channel Four crew."

"You hear right, Sergeant," said Kearney. "Let's hear your advice."

"Don't do it. Someone will get hurt. Maybe Shepard. Maybe a lot of people."

"I think you're right, Sergeant," whispered Kearney, "but there isn't a goddamn chance in hell I'd admit it. This is the way Hartz wants it. It's probably the way the mayor wants it."

Kearney moved past Lieberman and strode to the elevator.

"Worth it?" asked Hanrahan as Lieberman joined him, the last two on the elevator.

"Father Murphy, it was eating me. I had to get it out."

"Like confession, Rabbi," Hanrahan whispered, standing alongside Janice Giles. "Good for the soul. Haven't seen it do much for the body."

"You are in a grotesquely jovial mood, Sergeant."

"What do you know about Navahos?" Hanrahan had answered.

Now on the narrow stairway beyond the door, their bodies huddled in the near darkness, Lieberman, Hanrahan, Giles, Craddock, and Ballentine stood ready. At the foot of the stairs stood the brooding Nowitz and an armed and uniformed SWAT sniper, his rifle held ready but not pointed up the stairwell where the five people stood waiting for Shepard.

"Names, Lieberman," came Shepard's voice.

"Giles, Craddock, and Ballentine," said Lieberman.

"Abe, how long have you known me?" asked Shepard.

"We've been acquainted for about twenty-five, thirty years," said Lieberman. "But that's not the same as knowing you, Bernie."

"Tell Kearney to cut the crap," said Shepard. "Giles

63

works with a sound man named Nowitz or an old guy named Trout. There's no Ballentine at Channel Four."

"He's new," said Lieberman.

"If he wants to get old, he'd better not come through that door. You've got three minutes to get the right people up here or I start target practice. I know what Channel Four people look like."

Lieberman tapped Ballentine on the shoulder and pointed down the stairs. Ballentine went down, handed the recorder to Nowitz, who snatched it from him, and stood next to the sniper.

"You got it, Bernie," said Lieberman. "Open the door."

On the roof, Shepard motioned the dog back to the concrete barrier.

"When I open," he said, "the first one through is Giles, followed by the sound man, then the cameraman. When they get in, you close the door, Lieberman. And you stay out. Anything but that and we write new headlines."

"Open," said Lieberman.

"Tell Kearney he has fifteen hours."

Shepard cradled the shotgun under one arm and slid the metal bar across the curved steel plates. He had to strain and the bar screeched, metal against metal, the fingernail of an angry giant against a massive blackboard. When the bar clattered onto the roof, Shepard shouted, "Wait." He backed up to the concrete bunker, leveled his shotgun, and called, "Come ahead."

Janice Giles came through first, squinting into the sun. Nowitz followed her with Craddock in back.

"Stop there," called Shepard. "You, with the camera. Put it down."

Craddock knelt and placed the camera on the roof. Janice Giles looked at Shepard and willed herself not to blink, which she could do quite well. Blinking in close-up was a sign of weakness.

"Now," said Shepard. "Put the bar back in place on the door."

Craddock didn't hesitate, though he had trouble lifting the heavy metal and sliding it across.

"Okay," said Shepard. "The two of you strip to the waist, take off your shoes, and roll up your pants."

Janice Giles watched the men do as they were told. When they were finished, Shepard rose and stepped forward through the concrete barrier, the dog at his side.

"If you hurry," he said, "you can make the noon report."

5

Mayor Aaron Jameson of the city of Chicago had been not only the leading black mayor of a major city but one of the national leaders of the Democratic party. Some talked about four years as the first black governor and then at least a run at the presidency. He would be no young stallion by then, but he'd still be six years younger than Reagan when he was elected.

That was almost four years ago, before the last election when Aaron Jameson had made it back into office by a few thousand votes and just ahead of a grand jury investigation.

Not that Jameson had taken any of the high hopes seriously. He never really figured he had a chance at the governor's mansion in Springfield, but the talk didn't hurt.

What hurt was lunatics, black and white, like the one on television.

"Turn it up," Jameson said, leaning back in his leather swivel chair behind his enormous mahogany desk.

Ty Wheeler, tall, black, forty, bespectacled, a former Notre Dame wide receiver, and the mayor's administrative aide, turned up the volume and moved back to the chair across from the mayor. Wheeler made a church of his fingers and watched silently while the mayor, who had been on the wagon for almost two months, sipped a Diet Coke laced with nondairy creamer.

On the worn leather sofa against the wall Chief Marvin Hartz sat watching, unsure of whether to look supremely confident or massively nervous. He thought for an instant of the Fishery, his favorite restaurant in Key West, where he could stop for a beer and a cold grouper sandwich and talk to Pete Stowell about the bad old days.

". . . earlier this morning," Janice Giles said somberly, looking directly from the screen at more than a million people, "on the roof of the Shoreham Towers apartment building on the far North Side."

Giles spoke from in front of a police barricade, beyond which uniformed officers stood ready or kept the growing crowd back. The picture changed and there was Giles talking to a burly man with graying hair blowing in the gentle wind, a shotgun cradled like a baby in his arms.

"This shouldn't take long," Shepard said, his voice deep, controlled. "I came home in the middle of the night, found my wife in bed with a man. He went for a gun and I shot them both."

"Then," said Janice Giles, "you're claiming it was self-defense, unpremeditated?"

"Miss Giles," Shepard said softly, "I walked into my apartment with a loaded shotgun. Look around you."

Janice Giles turned toward the camera and motioned for it to scan the roof. The camera, and the eyes of the audience of Channel 4, found the concrete bunker, the pile of food and weapons, and the radio and bedroll.

"Kind of hard to call it unpremeditated," said Shepard as the camera pulled back to bring him and Janice Giles into view.

"Then why . . . ?" asked Giles.

"Young lady," said Shepard.

"Now he's everybody's favorite uncle," said the mayor with a sip and a sigh, glancing at Chief Hartz, who pretended to be so absorbed in the interview that he neither saw nor heard the mayor's sarcasm.

"This city," Shepard said, looking directly into the camera, "hell, the whole country, has been sliding down a rusty razor blade for years. My wife said some things when we got married. The fella I shot said some things when he got married. Nothing counts much anymore. You kill someone or sell them drugs that kill them and you walk away.

Women, married women, unmarried women, jump into bed with any guy they meet in the supermarket when they should be home . . ."

"Times have changed," Giles said with some irritation. "Women no longer . . ."

"They shouldn't have changed," Shepard came back calmly, sadly looking at the camera and not at Janice Giles.

"Hell," said Mayor Jameson, "he's better than that Republican clown they ran against me. If they'd run Shepard, the son of a bitch might be sitting here and I might be up on some roof with a mangy dog."

"I didn't agree to any damn changes," Shepard went on. "The way I figure it, wives stay faithful to their husbands and best friends stay loyal to each other and don't go around . . . getting in bed with their friends' wives . . . Am I keeping this clean enough for you?"

"Best friends?" prompted Giles.

"My former partner," said Shepard. "The newest captain in this town."

"Alan Kearney?" asked Janice Giles.

"Alan Kearney," Shepard confirmed. "The fair-haired boy of the department who's planning to marry into Chicago society, the man who introduced me to Livy—Olivia, my wife—and then turned her into a whore."

"And you want . . . ?"

"Kearney up on this roof at midnight, tonight. I want justice. You remember justice? Balancing the scales, making things right."

"Lieutenant Shepard," Giles said gently, humoring. "Do you really expect Alan Kearney to come up here and face you like some cowboy movie?"

Shepard paused, smiled sadly, and reached down to scratch the head of the dog.

"Dog's a stroke of goddamn genius," said the mayor, looking at Ty Wheeler, who sat staring at the television screen.

"Nothing like that," said Shepard. "I just want to talk to him, ruin his life the way he's ruined mine."

"And how are you going to do that?"

"Lady," Shepard said, nodding at the camera, "I've already started."

"And if he doesn't come?"

Shepard shrugged, a shrug of deep regret.

"Then," he said. "I blow up this building, myself, maybe a half a block or two of the lakeshore. And the city knows that Alan Kearney, if he were man enough, could have stopped it."

The roof was suddenly gone and on the screen was the familiar newsroom of Channel 4 with anchor Jim Amacor on the right and Janice Giles on the left behind a curved desk.

"In spite of the horror of his actions," Giles said, "the confusion of his ideas, you can see the pain and heartache in Bernie Shepard's face, and you can't help hoping that somehow he can be brought down from there with no one getting hurt."

"Fascinating story, Janice," Amacor said. "And what do the police and mayor's office say about the situation?"

Giles put her notes into a neat bundle.

"So far," she said, "the police have made no official comment, and the mayor's office is not responding to . . ."

"Turn it off," said the mayor, turning his swivel chair away from the television.

Ty Wheeler unchurched his long fingers, got up, and was at the television in two strides, turning it off.

"Why don't we just hire Shepard to handle our public relations?" said the mayor, laying his hands palms down on the desk. "He does a hell of a lot better job than Harley and his whole damned crew. You see that business with the dog? Man lives through this and he can run for goddamn governor. What are we doing about this?"

"We've got some options," said Hartz.

"That's reassuring, Marvin," said the mayor, looking at Ty Wheeler, who remained standing and gave no reaction.

"I've got men working on the door to the roof," Hartz

went on. "They're being very careful, very quiet, and that's going to take time. We can't get in close with a copter."

"I heard," said the mayor.

"But," said Hartz with cautious enthusiasm, "we can get in high enough to drop a small bomb or launch one causing minimal damage unless he really does have the roof wired."

"Does he?" asked the mayor.

"We don't know for sure," Hartz said.

"No bombs." Wheeler's voice came across the room. It was an impressive voice and Wheeler knew it. He had been, among other things, a late-night radio disc jockey. He had cultivated that smooth, decisive timbre, had learned to use it sparingly and at dramatic moments. It was a skill the mayor much appreciated.

"Remember the bomb in Philly took out more than that cult," Wheeler continued. "It took out Mayor Wilson Goode's political career. No goddamn bombs. How is it going to look if we blow up a whole block to take out one cop who caught his wife in bed with another man?"

Hartz felt at a disadvantage sitting. He got up, moved to the mayor's desk, ignored Wheeler, and said to Jameson, "If he's bluffing about having the roof wired, we can just wait and starve him out. We've got snipers ready if he shows himself."

Mayor Jameson folded his hands on his desk like a patient schoolteacher and looked at Ty Wheeler for an answer.

"That might take weeks," Wheeler said. "He has food up there. With the area off-limits to the public, we'll probably have over a thousand people kept away from their homes tonight. If this goes on for three days, maybe even two days, and doesn't end peacefully, we can have middle-class refugee camps or city payments for motels that could run into the millions. Every day he sits up there and we look up at him with our thumbs up our asses we lose votes. A week of this can swing the election. Son of a bitch picked Ryan Conners's ward to roost in."

"The primary is a month away," said Hartz, looking at

the mayor and seeing in his eyes that Wheeler was winning this battle.

"If it were tomorrow or the next day," the mayor said, "we could tell the voters that we promised to have him down with no bloodshed on the morning after the election. Then if we screwed it up, Marvin, you could resign and head for Florida and the public would have two years to forget Shepard, but this could turn into Aaron Jameson's last mistake."

"Look," said Hartz standing straight, "I'm—"

"—a political compromise," Wheeler jumped in, "a white concession to the police force and the people who didn't vote for us."

Hartz looked at the mayor for support, saw none, went for the look of anger, and tried again with, "I'm not—"

This time it was the mayor himself who cut him off. "What about Kearney?"

"Kearney?" asked Hartz.

"Might Captain Kearney decide or be persuaded to take heroic action," asked Wheeler, "if other options fail?"

"I can't order a man to go up there and face that lunatic," Hartz said with dwindling indignation.

"Of course not," returned Wheeler, moving to the mayor's desk and standing next to and half a head taller than the chief of police, "but a truly heroic and ambitious police officer who wanted to clear his name might well decide on his own to face the challenge."

Hartz looked at Wheeler and then at the mayor and understood.

"Captain Kearney is on the scene, in charge," Hartz said slowly, carefully. "We've set up a command post right across the street from the building. I'll go back there myself, get a full report from Captain Kearney, and remind him that I have made him fully responsible for handling this crisis."

"The buck stops as far down the line as we can send it, Marvin," explained the mayor. "That's politics."

"There is one other possibility," said Hartz. "A bit un-

71

conventional. One of Kearney's men knows someone who . . ."

"Take the initiative, Chief," said the mayor, rising. "I do not wish to know the details of the professional operation. You have my complete confidence. But have that talk with Captain Kearney about his moral and civic responsibility in any case." The mayor, standing now, picked up the phone on his desk. "It might be best to get things in motion as soon as possible," the mayor went on, and Hartz knew he was being dismissed.

On the way to the door, with Ty Wheeler as his escort and the cheerful laughing voice of the mayor behind him on the phone, Hartz silently cursed the day he had decided to back Aaron Jameson's political career.

When Abe Lieberman had left his son-in-law and his home two hours earlier, he had headed for the expressway, going ten to fifteen miles above the limit. He hit the Kennedy in eight minutes and got off at North Avenue twelve minutes later. Forty minutes from his front door he stepped into the North Avenue Station, from which he had been transferred more than a decade earlier.

Th North smelled just the way it had forever. Each police station has its own smell. It takes years to develop it and the final result is an unsubtle mixture of sweat, rot, mildew, drunks, forgotten burgers and pizzas, ancient doughnuts, and the tears of mothers and children. Ethnic changes also had their say. The North smelled vaguely of taco sauce and onions, a smell that, Lieberman decided, was a definite improvement over the past.

There were two people behind the bulletproof glass plate of the reception desk. One was a near-retirement uniformed bald egg of a man named Fullmeister. Fullmeister had been adjusting his collar for over thirty years in the hope that he would find the neck that was not there. The other person, also in uniform, behind the glass plate was a young Latin-looking woman with short no-nonsense hair and a serious look on her face.

"The Bloodhound returns," called Fullmeister.

"How you been, Sid?" asked Lieberman.

"Surviving the war, which is all you can expect out of life," said Fullmeister, adjusting his collar. "Hal's waitin' for you."

"What's he got?" asked Lieberman, moving toward the narrow wooden stairway to the right.

"Del Sol," said Fullmeister as Lieberman started up the stairs. "You talked to the X-man lately?"

The X-man was Xavier Flores, Lieberman's first partner, who had retired to Atlanta almost sixteen years ago.

"Spends his days at the zoo," said Lieberman. "Nights at the ballpark. His grandson Tony's a big lawyer now."

"I'm next," said Fullmeister. "Breaking in my replacement right now."

"Good luck," said Lieberman, going up the first stair.

Behind him Lieberman could hear Sid Fullmeister whispering, "Would you believe that little bastard beat the shit out of both of the Guttierez brothers right in front of All Saints Church on a Sunday morning?"

"No," came the incredulous voice of the Latin-looking woman.

The myth, thought Lieberman, going slowly up the wooden stairs. He had not beaten the shit out of the Guttierez brothers in front of All Saints Church a dozen years ago. He had stopped Manuel Guttierez, a drug dealer, a block away from the church and told him not to deal on Sundays. Guttierez, with his younger brother and Chinga Ramirez, had laughed at the little man with the baggy eyes who looked like a sad old dog. That had been a mistake. Lieberman had pulled his gun, stepped up to Guttierez, shoved the barrel into the man's gut and pulled the trigger. It clicked on an empty chamber and Manuel Guttierez had gone into seizure. He couldn't catch his breath. His brother and Chinga Ramirez had come to his aid as Lieberman raised his pistol and pulled the trigger. This time, within earshot of the All Saints Church, the weapon fired.

"You never know with these things," Lieberman had said with a whimsical shake of his head.

"El viejo es loco," said the younger Guttierez.

"Quisas," said Lieberman. "You don't deal on Sundays."

That was the way it had gone. It wasn't the only myth about El Viejo in the district. He was a legend who had gotten out just in time, before anyone tested the legend. He had traded Hispanic poverty on the near North Side for the far Northeast Side, Rogers Park, Edgewater, and a section of Uptown where the odds were even that a 545 call could turn up a Russian, Vietnamese, Hispanic, Southern white, Chinese, or Korean body.

Lieberman remembered these stairs, but they were higher and harder now. He had lost a little more cushion in his arthritic knees since the last time he made this climb. When he got to the top, he paused, not to catch his breath but to be sure his knees would not rebel and refuse to support him. It wasn't as bad as he feared.

The hallway was dark. It had been born dark in 1933, but Lieberman knew where he was and where he was going. He followed the voices in Spanish. They led him to the end of the hall, past the double door of the squad room, which he did not feel compelled to open for old times' sake. He had no impulse to look at his old desk in the corner near the cracked radiator.

Querez's door was closed but not locked. It was wood, windowless, and badly in need of paint. Querez's name was stenciled in white. Just above it, if one knew what one was looking at, was the name of the previous occupant which had been removed but had left an indelible shadow that only fresh paint could obliterate. The previous occupant had been Lieberman's old boss, Larry Doyle, cousin of a former fire commissioner. Captain Doyle had died in the line of duty shouting at a drug-dazed shoplifter, who had smiled as the captain grew ever louder and had a stroke.

Lieberman knocked at the door and Hal Querez answered, "Come in."

Lieberman entered. Behind the desk in the yellow-walled

room sat Sergeant Hal Querez, who looked vaguely like a thin George C. Scott, so thin, in fact, that he had to wear suspenders because he had no hips. Hal Querez also wore a perpetual smile that suggested that he had a secret. Hal Querez survived the insanity of his district by considering all of life a wonderful, horrible joke played by God. This was the secret he would gladly have divulged had anyone sincerely asked.

Across from Querez sat, or rather slumped, Emiliano "El Perro" Del Sol, who smiled at Lieberman. El Perro's smile was memorable, for his face was a map of wild scars leading to dead eyes. A scar from who knows what battle ran from his right eye down across his nose to just below the left side of his mouth. The scar was rough and red, and had probably taken an afternoon of stitches. The nose had been broken so many times that there was little bone, no cartilage. When lost in thought, which was seldom and most frightening, El Perro played with the flesh of his nose, flattening it with his thumb, pushing it to one side absentmindedly. His teeth were white but uneven, except for his sharp eye teeth, which had never grown down into place and made him look rather like a vampire. Emiliano's black hair was, as always, brushed straight back, and he liked to think that he resembled Pat Riley, the coach of the New York Knicks.

"El Viejo," said Emiliano, sitting up. "My men are getting a railroad here."

"I weep for you, Emiliano," said Lieberman, moving to the last chair in the room, a metal folding chair with the paint chipping to show the dull metal beneath.

"I appreciate that," El Perro said sincerely. "*Este puerco . . .*"

"What did I tell you?" Querez interrupted with a patient smile. "You watch your mouth, or you'll be learning sign language."

"I like him," said El Perro, pointing at Querez.

"We got two of Del Sol's gang on an armed robbery," said Querez. "Wertzel's TV on Crawford. Witnesses, even

75

videotape. One of them has a prior conviction, one of them has a pair."

"Hey," said El Perro, standing up and filled with indignation. "We ain't no gang. We're a club, Tentáculos. We do good stuff. You know that, Viejo. We play baseball. You want to see our bats and balls?"

"*Sientase*, Emiliano," Querez said, getting up from behind the desk.

"I think you should sit," said Lieberman.

Emiliano Del Sol sat and played with his nose.

"They got Fernandez and Piedras," said El Perro. "They wouldn't do a thing like that. You know that?"

Arturo Fernandez was a broomstick who always dressed in black and had a passion for very young girls. Piedras, whose real name was Jesus Montoya, was a violent hulk with no measurable IQ.

"How old are you, Emiliano?" asked Lieberman.

El Perro shrugged.

"You're twenty-eight," Lieberman went on. "The last time I arrested you, you were fifteen."

"You was the first cop to arrest me," said El Perro with pride. "When I was a little crap-ball maybe nine, ten, *verdad*, Rabbi?"

"What do you want, Emiliano?" asked Lieberman.

"You're on the Shepard shit, right? Cop up there on that building who blasted shit out of his wife and some cop?"

"I'm on it," said Lieberman.

"I know Shepard," said El Perro. "*Duro*, hard, thinks he is El Dios himself. You gonna have a hard time getting him down. People gonna get dead."

"Now I see," said Lieberman. "You've decided to go straight. You're going to be a news analyst and you want me to get you a job on the *Tribune*."

El Perro stopped playing with his nose and laughed. He looked at Querez who was still smiling, and then at Lieberman, who wasn't smiling at all.

"I can get him," said El Perro.

Lieberman and Querez said nothing. El Perro went on.

"When I was a kid, when you bust me I was the best burglar you ever seen, right?"

"You were talented," Lieberman admitted. "But you got caught."

"I was a kid," he said impatiently. "I ain't been caught since I was fifteen, not that I done anything, except that one time by Shepard, and I got out of that. But it took you to really catch me, Viejo."

"I'm honored," said Lieberman.

"You should be. Hey, I can do stuff cops can't do," whispered El Perro. "You know that. I go up there I got no rules."

"And in exchange for this gracious act of public service?" asked Lieberman.

"Fernandez and Piedras walk," El Perro said. "Innocent men walk."

Lieberman looked at Querez, who blinked his eyes slowly.

Silence.

"Pues, digame algo," said El Perro, looking at Lieberman.

Querez pushed a button on his phone and didn't answer. Less than three seconds later, two uniformed officers stepped into the room. Both of them were big. Neither was smiling.

"Find out where we can reach Mr. Del Sol if we need him," said Querez. "And escort him to the street."

El Perro stood up, looked at Lieberman and said, "I can do it, Viejo. You know I can."

When the two officers and El Perro were gone, Lieberman looked at Hal Querez.

"The way I figure it," said Querez, "off the record and it ain't my call, but what have we got to lose? That crazy shit goes up there, gets Bernie or gets himself killed."

"Fernandez and Piedras?" asked Lieberman.

"No one got hurt at Wertzel's. They didn't get away with anything."

"That the way you look at it, Hal, or the way you figure Hartz will look at it?"

"Abe, we got a choice here? If we don't let Hartz know about the offer and he finds out, you're back at the North and I'm ducking Uzis on the West Side. We're both too old."

"And you figure Hartz'll take it seriously?"

"He's gonna figure the way I said, 'What have we got to lose?' "

When he got back to the Shoreham half an hour later, Lieberman passed El Perro's offer on to Alan Kearney.

6

Alan Kearney surveyed the battlefield that had recently been recognizable as the stylish apartment of Dr. Jason Belding. Papers, phones, ashtrays, and empty junk food bags littered the tables, chairs, and floors. The white carpet showed dark and dirty indentations that might well be permanent. Two policemen were in the corner, one on the phone, the other filling in a log.

"You listening to me, Captain?" Alton Brooks said, breaking into his consciousness.

Kearney was sitting in a sofa, considering another coffee, but the idea turned his stomach. Brooks stood darkly over him, hands behind his back, waiting like Father Cronowyz at Saint Ignatius when a boy was brought up for discipline. Father Cronowyz, however, had learned the value of the pregnant pause, the long delay that set the prey on edge and made him ready to confess to any and all crimes in the hope of escape from those accusing eyes. Kearney had wondered if this was part of Jesuit training and if the Jesuits might be willing to take on the instruction of some Chicago police officers. Brooks would be high on the list.

"He's not going to let your men get a clean shot at him from below," said Kearney.

"I think you need a few hours sleep here, Captain," Brooks said in a lowered voice. "We're not talking about what he will or will not do here. We're talking about whether or not my men have the go-ahead to pick him off if they get a clean shot."

"You've got it, but you won't see him."

"And the door?" Brooks pressed.

"Hartz already told you to go ahead."

"To work on the door, not what to do when we can open it. It's your operation. I'm not getting into any blurred lines of command if something goes foul when this thing is over."

"Take the fucking door."

"We've got the ..."

Someone knocked on the front door of Belding's apartment. No one seemed to notice.

"Just be quiet and don't use the radio," Kearney said, closing his eyes.

"Kearney, who do you think you're dealing with?"

"Sorry, Brooks. It's been a long night and the day doesn't promise to be much better."

Whoever was knocking did it again, only louder, and the cop at the phone turned and shouted, "Just open the fuckin' door and come in."

Carla Duvier opened the door and stepped in. The policeman at the phone and the one at the log joined Brooks in looking at her. Her hair was drawn back in a tight bun and she wore no makeup. She was wearing a yellow skirt and vest and a white silk blouse.

Carla Duvier was accustomed to being looked at. Usually she liked it. Now she had business. She crossed the room to Kearney, who opened his eyes.

"Let's talk," she said softly.

"You've been watching the news," said Kearney, getting up.

"Is it true?"

Kearney looked around at Brooks and the two policemen, who weren't even pretending to do something else. Kearney nodded toward the bedroom door and led the way. Carla followed him as he entered, turned to the cop at the phone, and said, "Just leave the fucking door closed and stay out."

With that, she shut the door behind her and faced Kearney.

Jason Belding's bedroom had been reasonably untouched by Operation Seven. A few people had taken short rests on the bed, used the bathroom, but it could be saved. Alan Kearney wasn't so sure the same could be said of him. He turned to face Carla, who stood with her arms folded just below her breasts.

"It's true and it's not true," he said. "I knew Olivia before she married Bernie. I went out with her. I went to bed with her once, but it was nothing either one of us wanted to do again. Once. That was it and was before I introduced her to Bernie. After they were married, I stayed away from her, both of them, asked for a transfer and got it and a promotion."

"Then," asked Carla, "why is he doing this?"

Kearney felt the stubble on his cheek and lifted his arms.

"I'm not sure," he said. "He wants to blame somebody, anybody but Bernie Shepard, and it looks like I'm the somebody."

"And that's all?"

"That's all. I'm sorry. I'm not happy about it."

Carla moved forward and took his face in her hands.

"I'm not happy about it either, but we'll ride it out."

Kearney examined her beautiful face and saw the tension in her tight lips.

"And your father?"

"He doesn't watch television."

"He has other people who do it for him."

"I'll handle my father."

And with that, she kissed him.

"Brickass Brixton would love this weapon," Carl said, holding his rifle barrel up to the window. The sun shone down the ribbed tunnel, and Carl was happy. Chuck Norris, eat your goddamn heart out. Dave's rifle lay in his lap. He was breathing softly and watching "Divorce Court" on TV. He glanced down to watch the ice-cream bar tattoo on his chest ripple with his breath.

Dave McAulife was not too gung ho keen on this whole

plan, but he hadn't had a major thought of his own since he met Carl Binyon four years ago. Carl had talked him into the army, into coming to Chicago, into whatever shit they were about to get into. Now Dave was doing something that resembled thinking, and Carl didn't like it.

"What is so hard? I mean what is so goddamn difficult here?" asked Carl. "We had worse shit patrols in Saudi. Remember that town. Town, shit, that oil rig with the tin shacks? What was that called, Ali Khan, some shit like that? What did we get for that? Bumper stickers."

"That was a while back, Carl."

Carl put the rifle down, stood, and pointed at the television set.

"Did you see the TV? Were you lookin', Dave? With your eyes open?"

"I was lookin', but ..."

"But my ass," said Carl, pointing to his ass in case David in his newfound inquiring mood might have forgotten where it was. "We go up there, take this guy out, and we'll be fuckin' heroes. Interviews. Geraldo, Oprah, Donahue. Women. What'd that guy say on Joan Rivers? The *Enquirer*'ll pay two grand easy to interview us. Maybe there's a book."

"I don't think so," said Dave, looking at the window.

"You don't ..." Carl kicked a crumpled potato chip bag and shook his head in disgust. "We got no jobs, running out of money. Cops try to kick our butts out of here and call us pigs, and you don't think so. You got a better idea?"

The few ideas he had put together this morning had given Dave a headache. There was no way he could come up with something better.

"Well ... ," Dave said, giving in. "What the hell, right? I've got my shoes."

Carl nodded grimly, picked up the rifle, checked the action, and pointed to the rope ladder on the table next to the sink full of crusty dishes. Dave got up and moved toward the ladder. A thought started to come to him. He cursed it away and imagined himself on "Geraldo," Carl on one side of him, Hulk Hogan on the other, applauding when Phil introduced David McAulife, the Rambo of Chicago.

In the stairway, behind the steel door leading to the roof of the Shoreham Towers, Officer Anthony Spiza, drenched in sweat, worked the crowbar under the upper hinge while Officer Donnie Howell, one step below, sprayed oil on bar and hinge. They had a battery-powered lantern on the top step pointing up at the door. The lantern made Tony's dark face hollow-eyed. To Donnie Howell, his partner looked like a zombie in one of those Living Dead movies. Donnie's black face looked pretty much the same to Tony Spiza.

The smell of sweat, oil, and dust on the narrow stairway suggested that it might be a good idea to take a break and throw up.

Tony applied pressure, steadily, slowly, carefully. He and Donnie had been chosen for this honor because they were the strongest team on the North Side. Both worked out daily. Both had won departmental awards for weight lifting. Donnie had, before becoming a cop, been in the Golden Gloves, a middleweight. With a 32–2 record, Dancing Donnie Howell could have had a pro career, but he was smart enough to know that he would never have been a real contender, that he would have never made a big dollar.

The crowbar slipped, screeched along the door. They could sense the SWAT sniper, below them at the foot of the stairs, go tense.

"Goddamn," muttered Tony.

They held their breath and listened. They could hear nothing on the roof beyond the door—no dog, no man.

"Sweat," Tony explained.

Donnie handed his partner the now-dirty towel.

Sergeant Lieberman had asked them for an estimate of how long it would take to get through the door. Donnie Howell had instantly replied, "Twelve hours. We could do it in one or two with a little noise."

Tony had nodded in support of his partner, knowing that

Donnie had no way of knowing whether it would take six hours or six days. Donnie was ambitious. Donnie had a future ahead of him and Tony planned to ride along with him. If Donnie had said they could get through the door in three minutes and have Shepard tied and delivered a minute later, Tony Spiza would have nodded yes. He would have wondered if his life was about to fall apart. He would wonder if Donnie had gone nuts, but as his father, Dominick, had often said, you belt yourself to a torpedo and you ride it to the end.

When Donnie had given Lieberman the timetable, Abe Lieberman had answered, "Go ahead. No noise. When you're a fingernail away from breaking through, let me know."

"I can take this hinge with one or two busters," whispered Tony. "We're makin' so much fuckin' noise anyway, what's the difference?"

Donnie considered Tony's question and his future.

At the end of the corridor on the top floor of the Shoreham, as the crowbar had slipped, Carl and Dave had stepped through a stairwell door. Had the sniper not been focused on the dark space between Officers Spiza and Howell, he might have heard, seen, or sensed the two men behind him carrying rifles and a rope ladder.

Carl motioned to Dave and they stepped inside an alcove out of sight of the sniper. There was an apartment door in front of them, just as they knew there would be though they had never been up here. The layout on every floor of the Shoreham was exactly alike.

"What the fuck they doin'?" whispered Dave, listening to the painful, almost quiet screeching of the crowbar on the steel door.

"I don't know," whispered Carl. "Be quiet."

Carl took the chisel out of his pocket and handed his rifle to Dave. Timing his efforts to those of Spiza and Howell, Carl worked at the lock on the door in front of them.

On the roof of the Shoreham Towers, the dog looked up

at the door and growled, a slow, low growl. Bernie Shepard, who was sitting back, eyes alert behind dark sunglasses, snapped off the news on his radio, turned up the volume on his two-way radio as he got to his feet, picked up his shotgun, and moved toward the door.

"Who's on the horn?" he said into the radio.

"Lieberman."

Shepard hoisted the rifle with his right hand and hit the switch on the radiophone with his left.

"Lieberman, you've got ten seconds to tell whoever's working on that door to back off."

"Both of the men on that door are married," said Lieberman. "One has two kids. Tony Spiza. You know him?"

Shepard was on one knee now, the radio on the roof beside him, the dog facing the door. He raised the shotgun toward the door.

"That's one of the reasons I wanted you up here, Abe," Shepard said. "No lies, no bullshit. I know Spiza. I'll kill him or anyone else out there if that door comes down. You've got five seconds. This is over when I say it's over. Not when Kearney or Hartz or the mayor or the president says it's over. It's over when Kearney comes up here."

"I'm stopping it, Bernie," sighed Lieberman. "Listen."

The ten seconds had run out. Shepard didn't have to check his watch. He had learned to gauge time by his pulse, by the beating of his own heart.

"Spiza, Howell," said Lieberman. "Stop now. Pack up and come down to Operations. Answer."

"We read," came Howell's voice. "We're almost . . ."

"You're shut down," said Lieberman.

"Shutting down," agreed Donnie Howell, and clicked off.

"Got that, Bernie?"

"Got it, Abe."

"No promise that we won't try again," said Lieberman.

"I didn't ask you for any promises," said Shepard, standing. He was aware of a new sound from the door. And then the radio crackled with the voice of Captain Alton Brooks.

"Lieberman, what the hell is going on up there? No one, repeat, no one has the the authority for an assault, and you're breaking goddamn radio silence. Get those men back up there."

Shepard looked at the door, then at the dog, who had turned to the edge of the roof. He picked up the radio and said, "Good try, Abe."

"Bernie, you're dealing with free enterprise," said Lieberman. "Don't make things worse."

"There is no 'worse,'" said Shepard, turning off the radio and walking toward the edge of the roof, shotgun ready. The dog loped after him.

In the corridor of the top floor of the Shoreham, Spiza and Howell were throwing their weight against the door, not the door to the roof but the door to the apartment through which Carl and David had gone a few minutes before. The sniper had heard them. They had gotten the door closed as they heard the sniper's voice call to the two policemen on the stairwell.

When Tony and Donnie threw themselves at the door, Carl was already out of the window. Dave had pushed a sofa against the door, but this was a door to reassure the tenant, not to keep out the determined burglar. The door quivered.

"Move it, Carl," Dave called, and Carl moved it.

From the street below Alton Brooks looked up toward the roof of the Shoreham and watched a man with a rifle slung over his back climb out of the window of the top-floor apartment. The man had already flung a flimsy rope ladder up to the narrow crop of concrete just below the edge of the roof. He had done it with one smooth throw, as well as any of Brooks's men, better, but this was no one on his team. The man started to climb the ladder. Moments later a second man, smaller, also with a rifle over his shoulder and wearing no shirt, climbed out of the apartment window.

"Who the . . . ?" Brooks muttered and realized that his radio was on SEND.

Spiza and Howell hit the apartment door for the fifth time and felt the lock snap. Both men drew their weapons, and Spiza kicked at the door, sending the sofa squealing across the wooden floor.

The room was empty, but the window was open. Howell went for the window with Spiza at his side.

Alton Brooks was in a cold frenzy of hate and fear, hatred of whoever those two fools were who were climbing toward the roof, and fear that if they didn't succeed, Bernie Shepard might do something to make Brooks's team look very bad.

As the two men reached the ledge just below the rooftop and crouched down, another person, a black policeman with a radio, appeared at the window.

"Two civilians, armed," said Howell into his radio. "They may be going up there to join Sergeant Shepard."

"They're going up there to join their ancestors," said Lieberman with a sigh. "Call them back. Don't worry about making noise. Sergeant Shepard's listening to us."

Crouched on the ledge, just below the low wall of the roof of the Shoreham, Carl whispered to Dave, "Over and ready."

Dave didn't like it one bit.

"You two," came a voice below them. "Come down. Fast."

Carl went over, rolling in the gravel of the roof, and came up, weapon ready as he had been taught. Dave leaped over just behind him and moved to the right. Gravel tore at his bare chest.

Nothing in front of them. Nothing but a water tower beneath which was a low wall of gray concrete blocks.

Carl motioned at Dave for the assault and got to one knee. Before he could get to the other, the dog leaped over the low wall of concrete blocks, skittered across the roof, and hurled itself at Carl, sinking its teeth into his shoulder.

"Son of a bitch," Carl screamed, dropping his rifle and ripping at the ears and eyes of the dog. Dave turned his weapon toward the dog and Carl and then heard or sensed a figure rising behind the concrete wall. He tried to bring his rifle up as Bernie Shepard fired. The blast tore into Dave's face and chest, turning his ice-cream tattoo bloody.

At the blast, the dog let go of Carl's shoulder, dropped to the roof, and turned to Dave, who looked at his friend with a question in his torn face before he fell forward.

Carl whimpered once and reached in pain for the rifle he had dropped. The sun laughed at him as he leveled his weapon in the general direction of the figure beyond the concrete bunker. Bernie Shepard fired. Carl, sensing a second agonizing bite or shot in his torn shoulder, staggered back with a terrible scream and tumbled over the edge of the roof.

The dog stood looking from roof edge to Shepard, who came out from behind the barrier, a shotgun in his hands, and moved to the man he had just shot. He used his foot to turn the man, keeping his weapon pointed at the body. The glazed open eye convinced Shepard the man was dead. Shepard moved to the edge of the roof where Carl had fallen, leaned over with the gun balanced against the brickwork, and began to fire.

From the doorway of the Shoreham, Alton Brooks looked at the twisted, bloody body of Carl Binyon and watched as Bernie Shepard blew out the flashing lights of two parked police cars.

From where he stood he could see Abel Fernandez, his best rifleman, on top of the five-story building across the street. Fernandez was protected by a brick chimney. He looked in Captain Brooks's direction and gave a slow, negative shake to show that he could not get a shot at Shepard.

Brooks nodded back to show that he understood. Something came crashing down to the street, and Brooks knew it was the body of the second man. He had expected it. What he didn't expect was the fluttering sound that followed the body. Brooks took a step away from the doorway and looked up. Curling down as if it had life and purpose was the rope ladder. It caught a current of dry wind, changed direction slightly, and headed for an old Buick parked across the street. The ladder snapped into the roof of the car with a metallic thud and slithered to the street.

And then there was silence.

From the window of Jason Belding's apartment, Abe Lieberman, Bill Hanrahan, and Alan Kearney watched the purple comedy. The two bodies fell. The lights of the patrol cars went out. The ladder floated down. Two SWAT men ducked for cover behind a car. Lieberman sipped at his coffee and spoke without looking at Kearney.

Just before Shepard had come on the radio to give his warnings about coming through the door, Abe had been on the phone with Nestor Briggs, who had given him a long list of calls ranging from "don't call backs" to "urgents." The urgents included calls from his daughter, his son-in-law, and Jeanine Kraylaw.

"What'd she say?" Abe had asked about the Kraylaw call.

"He did it again," said Briggs. "This time it was something about how his sister disappeared five years ago."

"No direct death threat?" asked Lieberman.

"Didn't sound like it to me, Abe," said Nestor, "but . . ."

"I know," said Lieberman. "I'll get over there if I can get away. Todd, my son-in-law . . ."

And that's when Shepard's voice had crackled onto the radio.

Now, three minutes and two bodies later, Lieberman looked at Alan Kearney.

"You giving serious thought to going up there tonight, Captain?" asked Lieberman.

"I'm thinking," said Kearney. "What would you do?"

"Clear the neighborhood and tell Shepard to go ahead and blast," said Hanrahan. "Urban renewal."

Kearney was staring at Dave's body in the middle of the street.

"I don't like the idea of Bernie Shepard being gunned down up there with a bullet in his brain," said Kearney.

"Whatever he's done, he deserves an end. He deserves better."

"Meaning," said Lieberman. "He deserves you?"

"Meaning, I don't know what," said Kearney, forcing his eyes away from the window.

"You've got it backwards, Captain," said Hanrahan. "He wants you up there to put one in your brain."

The knock at the door was light.

"I'll take it," said Lieberman, moving to the door while Kearney and Hanrahan continued to stare out the window.

Lieberman opened the door on a good-looking young uniformed cop whose name he couldn't remember.

"Sergeant," said the cop, "this isn't a good time."

"I concur," said Lieberman.

"I mean," said the cop softly, looking at Kearney, "I was on my way when . . ."

"What is it?" asked Lieberman, guiding him back into the hallway outside of the apartment.

"It's about Olivia Shepard," said the young man as Lieberman closed the door.

The corridor was dark. The carpet soft and silent.

"I . . . ," he began. "She and I . . ."

"Keep it," said Lieberman. "What's your name?"

"Voyce, Raymond Voyce."

"How old are you?"

"Twenty-six."

"My daughter's ten years older than you," said Lieberman. "She asks for advice. I give her advice. She doesn't listen. I'm giving you advice, Raymond Voyce."

"But I've . . ."

"Are you a Catholic?"

Voyce looked puzzled.

"Yes."

"Then take it to a priest."

"I did."

"I've got a question," said Lieberman. "Who's your confession going to help? I mean your confession here?"

"I don't . . . ," Voyce started in confusion.

Lieberman put a hand on the young man's shoulder and turned him gently toward the stairs.

"Think about it, Raymond Voyce."

When he went back into the apartment, Hanrahan walked toward him and whispered, "Rabbi, no way I would go up there."

Lieberman looked at Kearney's back and knew that quite the opposite was true of Captain Alan Kearney.

7

In the office of the mayor of Chicago, Aaron Jameson and his assistant, Ty Wheeler, were eating sandwiches at the mayor's desk.

"Dry," said His Honor. "Too dry. Maybe we should keep a jar of mustard in the office."

"You don't eat here often enough to make it worthwhile," said Wheeler.

"And maybe I won't be eating here at all in two months if we don't take care of business with our rooftop moralist."

The mayor took a drink of beer from an amber bottle as Wheeler put down his sandwich and went to his briefcase. The phone rang and the mayor picked it up.

"No calls, Harriet," he said. "I said none unless . . ."

The mayor listened silently to his secretary as Wheeler sat up and handed him a neatly typed sheet of paper.

"Yes," said the mayor into the phone. "I see. Tell Chief Hartz I'll get back to him as soon as I can. No, I don't want to talk to Channel Four, Seven, Nine, any newspaper, any radio station, the pope, Jesse Jackson, or the president."

As he hung up the phone, he looked at Wheeler and said, "We're going to have to call a press conference. Our good sergeant Shepard, our rooftop vigilante, just shot two citizens who probably went after him to collect the reward. . . . Only there ain't no damn reward. What was that old cowboy movie with Gregory Peck where all the young guys kept trying to shoot him because he was so famous?"

"The Gunfighter," answered Wheeler. "If Chief Hartz's plan doesn't work, I suggest a simple statement of confi-

dence in Captain Kearney with your assurance that under no circumstances will you permit the good captain to go up on that roof."

Aaron Jameson examined the neatly typed sheet. He found a clear spot on the desk, reached for the fountain pen his daughter Sonia had given him for his last birthday, signed the sheet, and handed it back to Wheeler.

"Go ahead," said the mayor. "I take it we put a bit more pressure on Hartz to insure that Captain Kearney heroically and silently refuses my protection and keeps his rendezvous high above the city in the light of the full moon."

"The moon won't be quite full tonight," Ty Wheeler corrected. "It's starting to wane."

"Then we have some hope," said the mayor, examining his sandwich again and wishing for mustard. "He doesn't think of everything."

"Hartz is no problem," said Wheeler, placing the signed document in his briefcase and closing it. "He may not be capable of influencing Kearney."

Aaron Jameson had lost his appetite.

"Ty," he said. "Are you suggesting that I talk to Captain Kearney?"

"No," said Wheeler. "Only that you use your considerable powers of persuasion to inspire Chief Hartz to levels of rhetoric he has not previously been known to possess."

Jameson shook his head, swiveled in his leather chair, and looked out the window.

"Tell me something," he said. "Are we really better than Wojeckski? Are we really any damn better than the Republicans?"

Wheeler paused so long before he answered that the mayor glanced over his shoulder to be sure he had been heard.

"If I didn't think so," Wheeler said finally, "I wouldn't be doing all this dirty work to keep you in office. The city needs you, Aaron. You want to stay in office, there's a price to pay."

Wheeler stood, picked up his briefcase, and headed for the door.

"And," said the mayor, continuing to look out the window, "Captain Kearney's going to pay it. I wonder if he even voted for me?"

"You want me to find out?" Wheeler asked emotionlessly.

"No," said the mayor. "Just have Harriet issue that statement to the press. Press conference in the morning. Let's make it early, let the bastards suffer."

"Six?"

"Perfect," said the mayor. "If we get through this one, I owe you a dinner at Escargot."

"If we get through this one," said Wheeler with his hand on the door, "I'll gift wrap a jar of mustard and have it on your desk by noon tomorrow."

"I'll put in a call for Chief Hartz to be back here in an hour."

"You don't have much faith in his plan?" said the mayor.

"Do you?"

"I'm the politician, Tyrone. Why do you answer me with a question?"

"It's not a question of faith, Your Honor," said Wheeler, opening the door. "My job is contingencies."

Four months earlier, Frankie Kraylaw had been standing in the living room of his two-room apartment just off of Clark Street with one arm around his son, Charlie, and another around his wife, Jeanine.

They looked like they were about to break into a cheerful old song like "Side by Side." Frankie's grin was broad and looked phony, but Lieberman had the chilly feeling that the young man was sincere and maybe more than a little crazy. His wife and son winced in pain and Lieberman said, "I think you're hurting your family, Frankie."

Kraylaw, still grinning, looked first at his son and then at his wife. Wife and son smiled back at him, but there was no joy in their smile. The wife was young, with dark straw-colored hair, and wearing a loose-fitting dress. Her eyes looked puffy red from crying. The boy looked like his father. Straight red hair, green eyes, pale. He had a large "Sesame Street" Band-Aid on his forehead.

"No," he said, his straight reddish hair flopping over his eyes so he had to clear them with a nod.

"Let them loose," said Lieberman, stepping closer. "Now."

Kraylaw let out a short, sharp sigh and let his wife and son go. Jeanine Kraylaw led her son to the sofa near the window and sat rubbing his arm and watching the old policeman who looked like some kind of tired dog. She had the hope that Frankie wouldn't be able to fool this one.

"Neighbors say you've been making a lot of noise," said Lieberman. "Sounded like you might be beating your wife and son."

"I never," said Frankie, looking shocked.

"Did he hit you?" Lieberman asked Jeanine and the boy.

"Did I ever hit you, love?" Frankie asked with great sincerity. "Don't I love you?"

"Frankie, sit down," said Lieberman.

"He never," said Jeanine, her eyes following her husband, who moved to a wooden chair in the corner and sat.

"Never," agreed Charlie, looking at his father.

"There's been a misunderstanding, Officer," said Kraylaw. "We did make some noise, television too loud maybe. Laughing. Hey, was it last night Charlie fell over and hit his head on the table? Lot of noise, screamed something fierce. That right?"

Jeanine nodded and Lieberman turned to Kraylaw, who smiled, eager to help clear up this terrible misunderstanding.

"You got a job?"

"White Hen Pantry on Broadway," he said. "But I've got ambitions. Saving up. Well, will be saving up when we catch up on some things. Gonna get one of those ice-cream carts, or hot dogs or cookies. You can make money if you get the right spots. Be your own boss."

"The American dream," said Lieberman. "How about you and me go in the other room and talk."

"I've got no secrets from my dear ones," said Frankie Kraylaw, pointing to his wife and son.

At that moment Lieberman was convinced that he was dealing with a very dangerous and very crazy young man.

"Man talk," said Lieberman, gesturing for Frankie to come with him.

"You're not goin' to take me in there and beat up on me?" he asked, still sitting.

"Talk only," Lieberman assured him.

"God's truth?"

"God's truth."

"Then," said Kraylaw, standing cheerfully, "why not?"

The bedroom was small, a double bed against one wall, a battered dresser. The bed was made, covered by a worn but decent quilt. A large painting of Jesus with a halo hung on the wall.

"Where's the boy sleep?" asked Lieberman.

"With the angels," said Frankie, closing the door behind them.

"With the angels?"

"I mean by that," said Frankie, pacing the room, "he sleeps in the living room on the pull-out. I mean by that he is a blessed child, as I was." Frankie touched his own chest with his left hand and looked at the painting of Jesus. "You're a Jewish man?" he asked.

"I'm a Jewish man," Lieberman confirmed.

"I could tell," said Frankie with satisfaction.

"You indeed have great powers of observation. Listen, Frankie," Lieberman said with a sad smile. "Stop walking and listen."

Frankie stopped and looked at the policeman.

"I am all attention. But believe me, this has been an error here."

"That's the problem," said Lieberman. "I don't believe you. I want you to go over there by the wall and look at Jesus, gain inspiration while I go talk to your wife and son.

96

I don't want you to come out there. If you come out there, I'm going to consider your actions resistance of arrest and I'll handcuff you to the radiator. You understand."

"Yes, sir," said the happy Frankie. "But you are not a large man."

"I'm a small man with a large gun and some surprises. Get over there."

Frankie clapped his hands twice and moved to the wall.

"You know," he said, "people like me."

"I don't like you, Frankie," said Lieberman. "And I'm people."

Back in the living room, Jeanine and Charlie were still sitting. When Lieberman had opened the bedroom door they had both shuddered.

"He hit you?" Lieberman asked, but it wasn't really a question.

Jeanine looked at her son and the closed bedroom door and nodded yes.

"Tell me," said Lieberman.

"Can't," she said, stroking her son's hair and looking at the bedroom door. "He's listening."

Lieberman moved back to the bedroom door and opened it quickly. Kraylaw was standing no more than three feet away.

"Frankie, go in the toilet, now. Your last chance. Stay in there."

"You are the police and all, sir," he said. "But you really got no right."

"Toilet," Lieberman repeated.

"I'm of the law," he said, and moved to the bathroom.

Lieberman closed the bedroom door again and faced the woman, who seemed to have come to some decision.

"He hits us both," she said. "And he says he's gonna kill me and Charlie. Cut us up. Say we went back home."

Lieberman looked at the boy, whose eyes were now fixed on the floor.

"I'll take him with me," said Lieberman. "You pack your things and think seriously about going back home."

"He wasn't like this from the start," she said. "It's being here, the city. He thought he'd beat it, you know. But I think it's beatin' him. He's my husband. He's Charlie's dad. He works hard. I don't want to leave him. I just don't want him to hurt us."

"Mrs. Kraylaw," Lieberman said reasonably. "I think your husband may be mentally ill."

Jeanine Kraylaw looked up at him and smiled.

"The good Lord will help him, will help us. I believe that. I truly do."

"You mind," said Lieberman, "if I give the Lord a little help?"

The little help turned out to be an injunction against Frankie Kraylaw issued by Judge Foster Berrick, who also ordered two days of psychological testing. Frankie was pronounced borderline psychotic and released.

"Lieberman," Anita Sachs, the young psychologist who did the testing, had said, "the city is filled with psychotics. There may come a time when the sane ones will be outnumbered and will have to take over the asylums. When the time comes, I'll probably be on the outside looking in."

"Not enough to put him away?"

"Plenty," she had said, pushing her mess of dark hair back from her face. "But that's not the point. The only question the court wants answered from me is, How dangerous is he out there? And the court wants me to answer, He probably won't kill anybody, won't engage in a major felony. And that's what I answer if the person in questions hasn't already chopped up the entire fourth grade at the Roswell B. Mason Elementary School."

And that was it. Kraylaw had gone back to the bosom of his family and Lieberman had walked away with the near certainty that Jeanine and Charlie Kraylaw would not live out the year.

Now, four months later, Abe Lieberman stood drinking his fifth cup of coffee of the day in Jason Belding's apartment and wondering what Anita Sachs's profile on Bernie Shepard would look like.

"Where is he?" asked the chief of police, stepping through the door of the apartment.

Lieberman could see that Hartz had prepared himself for this entrance. His fresh uniform was neatly pressed. His cap was foursquare on his head. His hands were at his sides and his voice had dropped several decibels. He was followed by two officers in uniform, both on their best military behavior.

"Mayor's office just called for you, Chief," said Lieberman. "His Honor wants you back at City Hall."

Hartz nodded, resisting the urge to touch his brow for telltale sweat.

"Thank you. . . ."

"Lieberman, Sergeant Abraham Lieberman. He's over there."

Abe Lieberman pointed to a chair against the window. The chair was in shadows. The late afternoon sun hallowed it. Emiliano "El Perro" Del Sol leaned forward into the orange light, and Chief Hartz had to admit deep within himself that the little bastard had made a better entrance than he had.

There was no need for a battery of tests on Emiliano Del Sol. His violence was carved into his face. But Lieberman doubted that Del Sol was mad. When the sane folk took refuse in the asylums, El Perro would probably remain outside, pretending to be crazy.

El Perro's scar glowed red in the dying sun, pulling his eye open, giving his smile a touch of madness. He wore a black Greek fisherman's cap tilted forward over his brow.

"You know who I am?" asked the chief.

El Perro nodded, unimpressed, and removed his cap, smoothing down his hair.

"You know what I can do?" Hartz went on.

El Perro shrugged and said, "I know what you can't do with that gut. You can't do knee bends."

"I can see to it that those two pieces of garbage we're holding. . . ," Hartz began softly between his teeth.

"Fernandez and Piedras," said El Perro.

"Your two pieces of garbage," Hartz went on, "will do so much hard time you'll be a grandfather when they get out. If you live that long. And you . . ."

Hartz reached back and one of the officers, as he had been instructed, placed a file in the chief's hand as deftly as if he were a nurse supplying his confident surgeon with just the right scalpel.

"We've found some outstandings," said Hartz. "I think we've got enough to call them yours, depending how the judge looks at it. I'd say an easy five years."

El Perro looked at Lieberman and said nothing as Hartz flipped through the file.

"I just spoke to the arresting officers," Hartz went on. "Piedras and Fernandez could be looking at . . ."

El Perro laughed and stood up.

"Este hombre is un chiste," he said to Lieberman.

"What'd he say?" demanded Hartz.

"He said you're a joke, Chief," Lieberman translated.

El Perro turned to Hartz, moved toward him slowly. One of the two uniforms who had come with the chief stepped between them. Hartz moved the man out of the way and held his ground.

"My men walk," whispered El Perro. "I walk. I walk with two thousand dollars, cash money."

"No money," said Hartz aloud. "What the hell do you think I want you to do?"

"You want me to go up on that fuckin' roof and waste one of your own."

"Wait a minute," said Hartz. "I don't want any killing. You've got a reputation as the best burglar in the city. A building like the Shoreham, hell, you won't even work up a sweat."

"Yeah," said El Perro. "I just climb up there and talk Shepard into coming down."

"Well . . ."

"You don't mind if I take a blade with me, maybe two?"

"If that's necessary to make you feel comfortable," said Hartz, looking distinctly uncomfortable. "This is all informal. Off the record. You get no record. You get no credit. All we want is for you to get a good look at the roof, come back, and tell us if it's armed with explosives and where they are."

"And if I have to use the blade? Two thousand before I go up there."

Hartz went back to the file.

"Looks as if you resisted arrest in the winter of 1989 and Sergeant Shepard had to use a little force. Let's see . . . three broken ribs, a few lost teeth, and . . ."

"Two thousand or you get some other stupid asshole to go up there. Only you ain't got no other asshole besides the fat one you sit on or you wouldn't be talking to El Perro."

"Two thousand, you bastard," Hartz said. "I'll pay it myself, but I can't get cash until tomorrow."

"Then I'll take a check," said El Perro with a smile. "You're the fuckin' chief of police. I can't trust you, who can I trust? You know what I'm sayin'?"

"Okay," said Hartz.

"I disappear along with charges against Piedras and Fernandez."

"You get Shepard and you walk with the check. You miss him and . . ."

"I miss him and I don't need no fuckin' money. I need a body bag, but I ain't missing him. My car's parked on Sheridan, near Morse. Black eighty-eight Impala. License plate says 'Perro.' Bag in the backseat. How 'bout one of your *azulitas* get it for me."

El Perro pulled a set of keys from his pocket and handed it to the chief, who handed the keys to one of the two policemen. The policeman with the keys left the apartment.

"I'll write your check and you'll have your bag," said Hartz. "You mind if we don't shake on this?"

"I got two rules, man," said El Perro. "I don't rumba and I don't shake hands with no cops except Viejo."

Hartz looked puzzled.

"He means me," Lieberman explained.

The look from Hartz was less than complimentary.

"You go right away," said Hartz.

"I go when it gets dark," countered El Perro. "Suicide's against my religion, you know. Now I sleep."

Emiliano moved back to the chair at the window, put his hat over his eyes and leaned back into the shadows. Hartz turned to Abe Lieberman, who did his best to convey absolutely nothing.

"I'll be back," said Hartz, giving his best threatening look in the direction of Emiliano Del Sol, who gave every sign of being sound asleep or lost in meditation.

When Hartz and his two men were gone, Lieberman stepped toward the shadowed chair.

"How did I do?" said El Perro, taking off his hat and smiling broadly.

"You were charming. You gave an enormous boost to my career," said Lieberman dryly.

"De nada," said El Perro. "When I get Shepard, my rep will grow even bigger. Won't be a club—Los Negros, even the Chinese—don't know I took a cop and walked, especially Shepard."

"Emiliano," said Lieberman, moving behind the sofa to the window and looking out into the street. Dave's and Carl's bodies had been removed. He looked toward the top of the Shoreham and saw nothing. "I've got a puzzle for you. The devil always lies. However, when asked if he is the devil, he must answer truthfully. You encounter two men, one of whom you know is the devil and you ask the men the question, 'Are you the devil?' Both men answer 'yes.' How do you know which man is the devil?"

"I like this, Viejo," said El Perro, sitting up and fingering the long scar on his cheek. "The problem is, why does one of the men lie and say he is the devil if he is not?"

"That's the problem," agreed Lieberman.

"You thought this one up?"

"A rabbi, long ago in Poland."

"If the devil knows he has to tell the truth when someone asks if he is the devil," El Perro thought, "then if the devil is smart, he will always have with him someone who lies and says he is the devil. That way, the devil thinks, he is safe."

"So?"

"Easy, Viejo," said El Perro. "Shoot them both."

"You got it," agreed Lieberman. "If a man walks with the devil and lies for the devil, then treat him as you would treat the devil himself."

"You warning me about something here?" asked Emiliano, standing.

"Get some sleep," said Lieberman. "There's an officer in the kitchen and another one will be outside the door. You'll go at nine, okay?"

"Fine with me," said El Perro, sitting again and closing his eyes. "Maybe I'll dream a little about this man who walks with the devil."

In the back seat of his limousine, D. Wayne Duvier was looking out the window at the boxlike Patton Gym, which marked the northern edge of Northwestern University in Evanston. In a moment they would be passing the old lighthouse. Normally, the sight of his alma mater and the reassuring landmarks gave him some sense of stability, allowed him some respite from the constant pinpoint focus that his responsibilities required of him. Today he was aware only of the presence of his daughter next to him.

He made some remark about his sister Sarah and her plans for rebuilding her house on Hilton Head, knowing that neither he nor Carla was the least bit interested.

"This isn't working, Dad," Carla said.

"I suppose not," he agreed.

"We've got to talk about it."

It was moments like this that Carla reminded him most of her mother, his wife, now mercifully deceased. Rhea always wanted to face the truth boldly, openly, defiantly, directly, and if the truth didn't suit her, she would blame others, particularly Wayne, for altering reality and being insensitive.

"The policeman on the roof seems to have said all that really needs saying," he said.

"His name is Shepard," Carla said, making each word distinct, showing that she was working very hard at remaining calm and reasonable. "He is lying about Alan."

When her father continued to look out the window without answering, Carla insisted, "He's lying, Dad."

"Lying?" D. Wayne Duvier answered finally, turning to his daughter. "I don't think so. I recognize the conviction of the true believer when I see and hear it, and I saw and heard it on the news. Mistaken he may well be, but lying he most certainly is not. Besides, the media believe him and that, under the circumstances, cannot simply be ignored."

The massive white tower of the Baha'i Temple gleamed in the late afternoon sunlight. Wayne looked past his daughter and bore witness to its beauty, though he did not let it bear him away.

"I love him."

"And that, you believe is relevant? I once loved a girl named Gina who skated in the Roller Derby. And then there was a secretary whose name was, if I recall correctly, Thelma. Your mother and the course of time convinced me that I was not really in love with either Gina or Thelma. However . . ."

"I'm not going to let him face this alone," she interrupted.

She sat rigid, determined, her eyes fixed on his. Her face was lovely, her makeup perfect. The black dress and white pearls looked as if they had been purchased moments ago. D. Wayne Duvier knew the signs of victory, the last rigid set of the spine, the last threat, the last challenge before martyred capitulation.

"Then," he said, "there really isn't anything to discuss, is there?"

Carla shifted in her seat, turning her head angrily away from her father.

"I'm not abandoning Alan," she said.

"That," said her father, "is entirely up to you, Carla. You haven't needed my approval for the past decade."

Wayne reached over and touched his daughter's shoulder. As he anticipated, she shrugged him off and turned further away.

"Given your decision," he said, "would you prefer not to go to the Baker reception tonight? I'll be happy to make your excuses and I'm sure, given the situation, Anne and Sherman would understand."

"I'll go to the reception," Carla said, her voice filled with exasperation.

Wayne said nothing. He smiled, not a smile of triumph but a smile of bitter victory, which he was sure his daughter did not see.

Since Emiliano Del Sol was not going up on the roof of the Shoreham for almost three hours, Kearney had told Lieberman and Hanrahan to take the time to get something to eat and some rest. Kearney had spent two hours on Jason Belding's bed thinking of Navahos, dozing, listening to the voices in the living room. He had heard Chief Hartz come in, had heard El Perro, and he knew that he should get up, but he didn't. He had left it to Lieberman and now he owed Lieberman some time.

When Hanrahan and Lieberman were in the car, Hanrahan asked, "You ever been to New Mexico? Santa Fe?"

"Once, drove through. Looked nice. Why?"

"Navahos are from there, right?"

"I don't know."

"I've been thinking of vacationing there," said Hanrahan.

Lieberman didn't answer, so Hanrahan looked at himself in the mirror and touched his cheek.

"I need a shave."

"Use the electric," said Lieberman, pulling into traffic going south on Sheridan.

Hanrahan reached for the glove compartment, opened it, and pulled out a compact Braun razor.

"I need a real shave," he said, hitting the switch.

"I'll get you a real sandwich at Maish's," said Lieberman. "Today's Thursday. T&L Special's your favorite."

"Brisket?" asked Hanrahan over the razor's buzz as he tried to reach the little protected area just beneath his nose.

"None other," Lieberman confirmed. "And tonight it's on me."

Hanrahan clicked off the razor. He had more stubble to deal with, but he needed to be clear when he heard what was coming.

"Rabbi," he said, "what have you got in mind?"

"One stop on the way," he said as they passed the 400 Theater. "You ever see this *Rocky Horror Picture Show*?"

"No," said Hanrahan warily. "And I don't plan to."

"Father Murphy," said Lieberman with a sigh, "you are losing your youth."

"Where are you taking me, Abraham?"

"Kraylaws. There's a problem."

"God," said Hanrahan with an enormous sigh.

"God, indeed, Father Murphy," Lieberman agreed.

There were no parking spaces on Clark or on Albion, not even in front of the fire hydrant, where a van was camped. The alley off Albion was marked from telephone pole to brick apartment wall with signs in both English and Spanish saying NO PARKING: VIOLATORS WILL BE TOWED. There were no reasonable spaces in the alley. Lieberman pulled into an unreasonable one in front of someone's backyard. There was enough room for a thin human to squeeze through the gate. It was the best they could do.

The policemen walked around the building to Tío Coreles Muebles.

Less than an hour earlier, in a phone call filled with sobbing, Lieberman had been told by Jeanine Kraylaw that Frankie had broken up the furniture in their apartment a week ago. It had all been replaced in the last few days by Tío Coreles, who had felt sorry for Jeanine and Charlie

Kraylaw and had given her pieces of furniture he claimed he had been unable to sell.

Coreles's reward for his donation was a visit from Francis Kraylaw with a black metal bar. The ranting Kraylaw had threatened the old man with death, smashed five lamps and a vase, destroyed a wooden chair, and accused him of lusting after Jeanine.

The stop at Tío Coreles's was brief. The old man, shaken, was surrounded by soothing neighbors and family members. Tío Coreles had decided, he said, not to press charges. Instead he announced that he had taken on a junior partner, his nephew Antonio, a large man at his side of no great intellect but, both Hanrahan and Lieberman knew, possessed of a rap sheet that included two arrests for assault.

"I hope that crazy fool comes back down here again and tries something," Tío Coreles told the policemen.

Hanrahan and Lieberman went back outside and three steps north to the doorway that led to the apartments above Coreles's shop.

They opened the door and were hit by the musty smell of ragged carpet on the stairway. Lieberman pushed the bell next to one of the two mailboxes. They could hear the metallic ring above them.

"They're not here," said Hanrahan.

Lieberman looked at his partner with a sad smile and rang again. This time they heard footsteps on a wooden floor above and the opening of the door at the top of the stairs.

"Who is it?" came the voice of Frankie Kraylaw.

"Sergeant Lieberman and Sergeant Hanrahan," answered Lieberman.

"Jeez, oh. I've got to get to work and all. So if . . ."

"We'll just take a minute," said Lieberman, starting up the stairs.

"It's not a great time," said Kraylaw. "Not a great time."

"Tell us all about it, Francis," said Lieberman. "We are generally recognized as men of great compassion and understanding."

"What is it? I mean, why . . . ?"

"We happened to be in the neighborhood," said Hanrahan, "and we thought we'd just say hi to you and your fine family."

"You're always in the neighborhood," Frankie Kraylaw said with a false smile in his voice. "The station's two blocks away."

"Our thoughts were with you," said Lieberman. "As we drove by I said to Sergeant Hanrahan, 'William, let's pay our respects.' "

"I don't have to let you in," said Kraylaw.

They were standing in front of him now on the narrow landing. He had the door partly opened and they could see his smiling face, his red hair combed neatly back. He was a lean, good-looking young man, no doubt about it, but the bland look of madness flickered through his soul. Kraylaw was wearing jeans and a faded white button-down shirt with a frayed collar.

Beyond the door, Charlie Kraylaw whimpered.

Hanrahan pushed the door, sending Kraylaw scuttling backward into the room. Lieberman entered behind his partner.

A rusting window fan clanked behind the sofa in the cramped room. Lieberman sat away from it in an old but reasonably respectable green armchair. All the furniture was different from the last time Lieberman had been here. Now nothing matched in the room.

"You did some damage downstairs," said Lieberman.

"Downstairs?" Frankie repeated.

"Broke up the place," explained Hanrahan.

"I never," said Frankie sincerely. "Sergeant, you know I would never."

He reminded Lieberman of Anthony Perkins at the end of *Psycho*, sitting there dressed in his mother's clothes and thinking as he smiled, "I wouldn't hurt a fly."

The bedroom door suddenly opened and Jeanine Kraylaw stood there in jeans, shirt, and a frayed windbreaker, clutching her son and a black patent-leather purse and a small battered suitcase.

"We're ready to go," she said, not looking at her husband, pulling Charlie's head to her side.

"Jeanine," said Frankie, looking at her and then the policeman. "What are you . . . ?"

Hanrahan moved to intercept Kraylaw as he moved toward his wife and son.

"What happened?" asked Lieberman.

And she told them a tale of constant threats from her husband and his joy in telling her about the "disappearance" of people who had "troubled him," including his own sister Rachel.

"He told me something had happened to them in their sleep," she said quietly, frightened, not looking at her husband. "He was always different. He was always smart. But I think failure has made its mark on his brain."

"You think he might kill you?" Lieberman asked.

"And Charlie," she added. "He doesn't think Charlie is his."

"I never said . . ." Frankie began, and tried to move around Hanrahan, who grabbed him firmly by the arm.

"Is he?" asked Lieberman.

"No one else's he could be," she said.

"There's a blue car parked in the alley. Police sign in the window," said Lieberman. "You and Charlie take your things and get in the car. Pack what you need."

"You can't," said Frankie. "My family . . ."

". . . is going to be just fine," said Hanrahan.

When the woman and boy had left, Lieberman and Hanrahan took Frankie Kraylaw out for a walk and a Coke at the I-HOP. The conversation was brief and the warning clear. For an instant Frankie Kraylaw did not take the warning seriously. But that instant passed quickly. Lieberman took his gun from his holster and placed it on the table. Frankie Kraylaw grinned and looked at Lieberman, who sipped his coffee.

"How many people have I shot, William?" he had asked.

"Four," Hanrahan answered.

"Why?" Lieberman asked, watching Kraylaw's eyes.

"Combination of things," Hanrahan answered with a small shrug. "Harris was an anti-Semitic comment. The other three, all abuse cases, wife abuse. Spainner, Kleitman, Harley."

"Why am I particularly concerned about abuse of wives?"

"Because your mother was beaten to death by your father," Hanrahan answered emotionlessly.

"And what is your position on this issue?" Lieberman continued.

"Hell, you're my partner. You cover for me. I cover for you."

"You're bluffing," Kraylaw said.

Lieberman picked up the gun, aimed it just past the grinning face, and fired.

The sound both froze and deafened Kraylaw.

People turned toward the explosion and Hanrahan slipped out of the booth to calm them.

"Accident," he said. "Police. Blanks. Nothing to worry about."

Lieberman put the pistol back in his holster and took a slow sip of his coffee.

"Good coffee," he said. "Bad company. Are you capable of hearing me, Kraylaw?"

Frankie Kraylaw's grin was gone. His face was pale. His eyes were wide and fixed on Lieberman as Hanrahan returned to the booth and said, "Either of you two want another round of coffee?"

"You're crazy," said Kraylaw.

"I just told you that," Hanrahan said as if talking to a very slow fourth-grader.

The bullet had been a blank, and Hanrahan's story was one of many they had told over the years. Abraham Lieberman had never shot anyone. Abraham Lieberman's father, who had died at the age of ninety-two, had never so much as spoken a harsh word to his wife in over sixty years of marriage.

"You are harassing me," said Frankie Kraylaw.

"No," said Lieberman. "We tried that. It didn't work."

"I have not laid a hand on her. I have not threatened her."

"You told her stories," said Lieberman.

"I told her . . . Is that a crime?"

"You told her stories to frighten her," said Lieberman. "To make her think you might kill her."

"This is nuts," said Kraylaw.

"I agree," said Lieberman. "Chicago has not been good to you, Francis, but luck has finally smiled upon you. You have won exactly"—Lieberman opened his wallet and counted and then looked up at Hanrahan, who held up two twenty-dollar bills—"forty-three dollars in the Clark Street Take-a-Trip-on-Greyhound contest. I suggest you go pack a bag, catch the El downtown, and take the first bus out of the state."

"No," Kraylaw said, turning to Hanrahan. "We can't just . . ."

"Not 'we,' " Lieberman corrected. "You. Just you."

Kraylaw began to pace, but there wasn't much room.

"Who do you think you are? Telling a man he has to get out of town like some . . . some . . . cowboy movie. You're no sheriff. You've got no right."

"I'm going to tell you a story, Francis. It's not a long story. I've been a cop for more than thirty-five years. I've seen women, kids come and ask us for help. A father, boyfriend, uncle, neighbor they're afraid of. We go and give the guy a scare. Sometimes it works. Sometimes it doesn't and someone gets hurt."

"This is illegal," Kraylaw shouted.

"Walk on down the street," said Hanrahan. "Our captain's name is Kearney, Alan Kearney. He's a little tied up today, but he should be in in the morning. You just wait for him and tell him what we said. Your file will be on his desk waiting before you get there. My guess is he'll congratulate you on your good fortune."

"Not every day a man wins the Clark Street Take-a-Trip-on-Greyhound Contest," said Hanrahan enviously.

"This is America," Kraylaw cried. "My rights . . ."

Lieberman took out his pistol and placed it on his lap. "You've got a point. You don't want to go. No one can make you go. Money will go back in the pockets of the generous donors who cannot be counted on to renew the offer. They have been known in the past to come up with alternate packages, which, I'm sorry to say, some of the winners find far less attractive."

Kraylaw looked at the two policemen. He wasn't smiling. Neither were they.

"I'll have to go back to the apartment, pack my things," said Kraylaw.

When they were back at the apartment, Kraylaw went into the bedroom, leaving the policemen alone in the living room with Tío Coreles's furniture.

"Went pretty far with this one, Rabbi," said Hanrahan softly.

"Give me the odds on him hurting her or the boy?"

"I don't know. Fifty-fifty maybe. He's a mad one."

"Maybe one of us should help him pack while the other one figures out where she and the boy can go."

"My son Mike, the one in Buffalo. Maybe I can give him a call and he can give her a job in the insurance company."

Lieberman moved to the bedroom door, and Hanrahan ambled to the front door.

"I'll meet you in the car," said Hanrahan.

There was a chance, a slim one maybe but a chance, that Hanrahan would run across Clark Street and into one of the three bars on the block for a drink. Lieberman considered saying something, considered walking to the window to see if his partner went into a bar, and then decided that it was none of his damned business.

He moved to the bedroom and opened the door. Frankie

Kraylaw was throwing clothes into a big khaki duffel bag. He was also doing several things Lieberman did not like. He was smiling and he was singing. Not exactly singing, since Frankie didn't seem to know the words, but hum-singing.

Lieberman leaned against the door, arms folded, and watched lazy-eyed as Frankie became more frantic. His singing grew louder, faster. His smile broadened, and each time he threw a shoe, a mismatched pair of socks, a crumpled shirt into the bag, he looked at Lieberman.

"Enough," said Lieberman softly.

Kraylaw ignored him and grew even more frantic.

"Enough," Lieberman repeated. "It's full."

Frankie Kraylaw looked down at the bulging bag, a battered tennis sneaker in his hand.

"I am not satisfied with this," said Kraylaw.

"You don't have a vote," said Lieberman. "Zip it up and let's go."

"This is not fair. As God is my witness, this is not fair. This is not just. This is not legal."

"But it is right," said Lieberman.

8

It was almost nine, just before closing time, when Lieberman and Hanrahan hit Maish's T&L Deli. There was a lone unfamiliar face at the counter, a hunched-over man about forty in a cowboy hat. At the front table, three Alter Cockers—Herschel Rosen, Syd Levan, and Howie Chen—sat nursing tea and rye toast.

"A late night raid," said Herschel, who was widely accepted as the clan comic. "Quick, Howie, put away the opium."

"No, Hersch," said Howie straight-faced, "tonight it was poppy seed *haman tashen*."

Syd Levan, the youngest of the Alter Cockers at the age of sixty-eight, threw up his hands in a what-am-I-going-to-do-with-these-people gesture and added, "'Now, we confess the minute they walk in? We don't even wait to be tortured?"

Abe and Hanrahan moved to their favorite booth in the back where Lieberman could see the door and Hanrahan could look at the wall where a faded color poster cried out the glories of a sandwich made with Vienna red-hots and drenched in mustard, onions, and relish.

"Syd," said Abe wearily, "I told you before, if you want to be tortured again, you'll have to pay double. Things have been slow in the police extortion business."

"You get the joke with the *haman tashen*?" asked Chen with a satisfied smile.

"Even I got the joke," said Hanrahan.

"Notice how they stay away from me?" Herschel asked

114

the hunched-over cowboy, who nodded and went on eating. "Even the police fear the wit of a true Rosen."

Behind the counter Maish, whom nothing ever bothered, wiped his hands on his apron and said to his brother, "Coffee, Abe?"

"Coffee," agreed Lieberman. "What's hot and special?"

"The Atlanta Braves and the corned beef," answered Maish soberly.

"Hear that? What? Listen," said Herschel Rosen. "Now even Maish is trying to be a stand-up. How am I supposed to make a living in here with all the competition?"

"Shit," the cowboy said, throwing down a few bills. "Man can't go anywhere for a quiet coffee and hot dog without a bunch of dumb . . ."

Before he could finish, Maish picked up the bills and held them out to the cowboy.

"It's on me," he said.

"Generous Jews," said the cowboy, adjusting his hat but taking the bills. "Now I've seen everything."

"No you haven't," said Hanrahan, standing up. "You haven't seen the inside of your asshole, but we can take care of that omission right now."

The Alter Cockers were silent, enjoying the showdown.

"Gunfight at the Okeydokey Corral," said Herschel.

"High nine o'clock," added Howie Chen.

The cowboy stuffed the bills into his pocket and smirked. He was lean and possibly a little drunk.

"My pa didn't raise a fool for a son," said the cowboy. "I don't fight with cops. I just wandered in here by mistake."

"Cowboy among the Indians," said Syd.

"The lost tribe," Herschel added quickly, not to be one-upped by his straight man.

"Afraid we might scalp him," said Howie.

The cowboy lifted his hat to reveal an almost bald head.

"Genetics beat you to it," he said without cracking a smile.

"Stranger," said Abe Lieberman, "have a nice night."

"I'm driving straight through to Cleveland," said the cowboy.

"You're not from Texas?" asked Chen.

"Cleveland," said the cowboy, adjusting his hat and moving to the door. "Had a few too many beers. Sorry."

"You believe that, Abraham?" asked Hanrahan as the cowboy walked onto Devon Avenue.

"I believe in both God and the devil," said Lieberman, "and sometimes in our business I think they are in cahoots."

"I'll have a hot dog with everything," said Hanrahan, sitting down.

"One hot dog?" asked Maish, clearing the cowboy's plate and coffee mug.

"He's on a diet," explained Lieberman.

"Ah, a lady in the poppy seeds," said Herschel.

"Is she Jewish?" asked Howie Chen.

"Chinese," said Hanrahan.

Syd and Herschel laughed as if a joke had been made at Howie's expense.

"Another comedian is heard from," said Chen.

Neither Lieberman nor Hanrahan tried to correct them. Maish disappeared behind the short-order counter, and the policemen settled back in the hope of a few minutes' peace before they had to get back to the Shoreham.

"The guy on the roof?" asked Levan. "What's gonna happen? No joke?"

"We're going to get him down," said Lieberman.

"I know. I know," said Levan impatiently. "He could die of old age and you could carry him down with the start of the next century. That's not what we want to know. We got a special connection here. A source. We wanna go home and brag what we know before the television or the morning papers."

"Rabbi," said Hanrahan softly, "maybe we didn't pull a trigger, but what we did to Frankie Kraylaw maybe isn't a hell of a lot different from what Bernie Shepard did to his wife and Andy Beeton."

"It bother you?"

"What we did to Kraylaw? No."

"It bothers me," said Lieberman. "But I can live with it. Consider the alternatives. No, you want to know what bothers me?"

"Del Sol," said Hanrahan.

"You know me well, Father Murphy."

"Well, Rabbi, look at it this way. If we get him down, he does time, a lot of time. Bernie Shepard is no kid. And a cop, especially a cop like Bernie, slammed . . . Well, maybe he's better off with El Perro."

"That the way you'd want it?" asked Lieberman.

"The way I'd want it," said Hanrahan.

"That doesn't make it right."

"Doesn't make it right at all."

Maish returned with coffees for Abe and Hanrahan and placed them on the table.

"Yetta all right?" asked Abe, taking a sip.

"Of course she's all right," answered Maish. "She's not a spring chicken, but . . . You're not working Saturday, why not bring the kids over? I'll ask my Sam to bring Heather and David so they can play and we can talk."

"If he's off the roof, we'll see," said Lieberman.

"You're welcome too," Maish said to Hanrahan.

"Thanks," said Hanrahan. "But . . ."

"You bring your Chinese lady," said Maish. "My daughter-in-law speaks Mandarin, learned it at the University of Chicago. They'll talk. Your lady speak Mandarin?"

"I don't know," said Hanrahan. "I'll ask her."

"There's Cantonese and there's Mandarin," explained Maish. "Howie speaks Cantonese, right, Howie?"

Howie answered in Cantonese, which earned him a pat on the back from Herschel.

"What'd I tell you?" said Maish. "Think on it."

"Think Kraylaw'll come back?" asked Hanrahan softly when Maish moved away to check on their food.

They had driven Kraylaw all the way downtown, bought his bus ticket, and waited to put him on the first bus south with a bag of Chee-tos and a Frank Roderus paperback western, *Mustang War*. Then they had gone back to pick up a few things for Jeanine and Charlie Kraylaw and take them to Hanrahan's house in Ravenswood. It was temporary. The house was big enough. Bill and Maureen, who had left him four years ago when the drinking had been as bad as it had been in twenty years, had raised two sons in the house. Now the house was empty, which, normally, suited Hanrahan well enough.

The stay in the hospital had helped him step away from the bottle. It hadn't done long-term wonders for his head, but God, whom he was starting to talk to again, sometimes made strange and incomprehensible deals.

The agreement was that Jeanine would take care of Hanrahan's house till she decided where she wanted to go. Truth be told, Hanrahan was an excellent housekeeper, an almost obsessive housekeeper, since Maureen had left him. For the first two years he had kept it immaculate in the hope that she would come back and be delighted. For the next year he did it so that if she came back, she would see how well he was doing without her and be miserable. For the last year, he had simply done it because it had become a habit that he couldn't break, just as placing his football helmet on at exactly the same spot and angle had been essential during his high school and college playing days.

"He'll come back," said Lieberman. "If he were just mean and stupid, he'd stay away, but he's crazy and a little smart. He'll be back."

"He'll be back," agreed Hanrahan. "You think Bernie Shepard's crazy too?"

"Ich vais?" said Lieberman with a shrug. "Yiddish lesson for the night, Father Murphy. It means 'who knows.' Who knows what a person will do when they love and hate at the same time? Bernie, Kraylaw, my son-in-law Todd?"

Lieberman touched his bristly mustache for stray hairs and smoothed it down.

"Yeah," said Hanrahan.

Maish brought the sandwiches and the two policemen ate

silently, listening to the Alter Cockers argue the merits and demerits of *Once upon a Time in America,* the movie they had seen at the JCC that night.

After they ate, Lieberman looked at his watch.

"Time," he said.

"Time," Hanrahan agreed with a great sigh.

"How's your head?" asked Lieberman.

"It's fine, Rabbi, fine."

They got up and walked past the Alter Cockers.

"Abe," Herschel called.

Lieberman and Hanrahan paused to let Herschel have his joke.

"What is it, Herschy?" asked Lieberman.

"You and and the Irish be careful."

"Yeah," echoed the Alter Cockers.

". . . don't know where he is," said the officer on the phone in Jason Belding's apartment. "He was here half an hour ago. . . . Sure, I told Captain Kearney who you were. He wouldn't lie to a reporter. He has too much respect for the press."

Across the room Alan Kearney, in shirtsleeves and tieless button-down blue denim shirt, decided that it was dark enough. His eyes moved down to the seated Emiliano Del Sol, who wore a fixed deadpan look.

"Something on your mind, thief?" asked Kearney.

El Perro's eyes locked on the policeman and said nothing.

The policeman on the phone went on, "No, I don't think anything. Nobody here thinks anything. Chief Hartz does all the thinking. He's a god to us. . . . I told you he isn't here. What do you want? You want me to swear? Swear on the Bible? Okay, I fuckin' swear on the Bible. . . . Sure, you can quote me, go ahead and quote me. You don't even fuckin' know who I am. I'm a bum who wandered in off the street. My eyes are going bad. I'm half drunk and almost ninety and even I can see that Captain Kearney ain't here."

"No way in hell you're going to take Bernie Shepard," Kearney almost whispered to Emiliano.

El Perro smiled and stood, eyes still on Kearney.

The cop on the phone looked at the interchange with interest and went on to the reporter, "Okay. You got me. My name? Steve Carella, Eighty-seventh Precinct. . . . That's a coincidence. . . . Complain to your alderman. . . . Yeah, yeah. . . . Put it in a doggie bag and sleep with it."

The cop hung up with that and gave his full attention to the drama across the room.

"You've got a good act, Emiliano," said Kearney. "But this is Bernie's show."

"Hey," said Emiliano, "how come you ain't on my side, New Captain? I'm doin' your work for you, man. I don't come down with Shepard's skin, and you get to go up there next. You wanna take that walk, policeman? You feelin' guilty about somethin'?"

"You're not my idea, thief," said Kearney.

"Man," said Emiliano, "I was no one's idea, not my mama's, that's for damned sure. I ain't no one's idea. I'm their fuckin' shadow."

Kearney and El Perro were almost nose to nose when the door opened and a uniformed officer stepped in with a gym bag in his hand. El Perro lost interest in Kearney, stepped past him, and took the bag from the officer.

"You get lost?" asked Emiliano Del Sol. "Whyn't you ask a cop?"

Before any of the officers in the room could answer, El Perro was inside the bedroom and had closed the door behind him. He took one step into the room and allowed himself a massive grin and a touch of his scar. Yes, no doubt about it, El Perro was enjoying himself. All he needed were some of the Tentáculos watching him, some women. He would tell them all about it later.

The bathroom was dark. El Perro found the switch, put down the toilet seat, and placed his gym bag on it. He opened the zipper slowly to begin his ritual preparation for a job. As soon as he opened the bag, he knew why the cop had been late in bringing it. There was a sealed envelope on the top. Emiliano could feel that it contained money, cash. Hartz had turned out to be too smart to give El Perro a personal check with his name on it, a check to a professional thief. He wasn't even tempted to open it. Two thousand dollars was nothing. The only reason he had asked for money was to make the fat cop Hartz crawl like a roach.

He put the envelope aside and removed a pair of black pants and a black shirt. He took off his clothes, put on the pants and shirt, and checked himself in the mirror.

Good, good, he thought and patted down his hair before putting on a black knit hat. Finally, lovingly, he removed two sheathed knives from the bag, put them down gently on the ledge above the sink, and checked each knife for balance.

Holding one of the knives in his right hand, El Perro picked up one of Jason Belding's yellow monogrammed towels and threw it in the air. The towel landed on the knife and was severed in two without the slightest flick of El Perro's hand or wrist. Satisfied, he returned the knife to its sheath. He removed the second knife, held it up to the fluorescent light over the sink, examined it closely, put his ear next to the blade, tapped the blade with the nail of his small finger, and listened before slowly returning the knife to the sheath. Next, he hooked both sheaths to his belt and put on a lightweight black sweater. Only then did Emiliano "El Perro" Del Sol smile at himself in the mirror and whisper, "A fuckin' shadow."

When El Perro returned to the living room, Lieberman and Hanrahan had returned and were talking to Kearney.

"How do I look, Viejo?" asked El Perro.

"Brandon Lee would weep with envy if he could see you," said Lieberman.

Hanrahan, the big Irish, shook his head and Kearney turned to the window.

"Think so?" asked Emiliano seriously.

"Do it," said Kearney savagely, his back turned.

* * *

On the roof of the Shoreham Towers, Bernard Shepard stood looking up at the first light of the night stars. He knew nothing of the stars and couldn't remember ever having simply looked up at them, even as a kid. The stars did nothing for or to him. They were too distant, unreal. He had the feeling deep within him, a feeling he didn't deny but didn't want to let loose, that if he allowed his thoughts to drift to the sky, he would be panicked by the vastness, he would feel himself growing small, so small that he did not exist. He stopped looking at the stars and finished the can of tuna he had been eating. He wiped the fork on his shirt, tucked it into his pocket, and flung the can over the side of the roof and into the night. The dog looked up from his own open can as he heard the clink of metal on the street beyond, and then he returned to his meal.

Bernie Shepard moved to his bunker and looked at the green glowing dials of his watch. Then he adjusted the radio. There was nothing there but static.

He sat beneath the rusted water tower listening to static and the lapping of the dog's tongue and tried neither to think nor to look out at the vast sky.

9

In the lobby of the Shoreham Towers, Lieberman and Hanrahan walked with El Perro between them to the open elevator. The officers on duty inside the lobby stopped talking and watched the three men. When they reached the elevator, El Perro entered and turned with his hand out like a traffic cop.

"Far as you go," he said.

Hanrahan grabbed El Perro's sleeve, but Lieberman reached up and gently removed it.

"End of the line for you," said El Perro, slowly smoothing his sleeve where Hanrahan had touched him. "I got things to do I don't want no cop seeing. You know, like trade secrets. Seven minutes, man; remember seven minutes and you get on that radio—you, Viejo. You pump it up loud and give the man up there a story."

"Like what?" asked Lieberman.

El Perro reached for the elevator button.

"Like what?" he said, pausing. "Like I don't know. His old lady ain't dead. He just won the lottery. You got a lot to say. You got the tongue. You'll think of something. I got more faith in you than I do in Jesus Christo."

"I don't know, Zorro," said Hanrahan sarcastically. "Abe starts wailing like an African-American disc jockey and Bernie will know something's coming down."

"Hey, stop jerkin' around, man, and do your job. Lieberman knows what to do."

"Let him go, Bill," said Lieberman.

"You got it," El Perro said softly, pushing the button

now. The door began to close. "It's my ass hangin' up there on the fuckin' moon and the man up there with a dog and a machine gun."

Hanrahan reached in and held the door open.

"Makes you stop and think, doesn't it?" he said, checking his watch. "You've got six minutes."

El Perro laughed.

"You fuck this up and I'm gonna find you. I'm gonna find you and string your guts on your mama's clothesline," said El Perro.

Hanrahan continued to hold the elevator door open.

"My mama has a GE washer-dryer. I bought it for her with the money I took from the bodies of dead thieves."

Hanrahan pulled his hand back and held up his watch as the doors closed slowly.

"El chingo tiene cojones," came El Perro's voice.

Lieberman and Hanrahan watched the lights above the elevator indicate the floors. One, two, and then three. The light did not go on for four. The elevator had stopped at three. Hanrahan looked at Lieberman.

"The night is full of surprises, Father Murphy."

"That it is, Rabbi. You gonna mesmerize Bernie while your buddy cuts his throat?"

"Consider the alternatives," said Lieberman.

Shepard leaned against the rusted leg of the empty water tower. Darkness had come quickly. The full moon was bright. Shepard adjusted his radio, but there was only the soft hum of static. Lying a dozen feet in front of him, the dog opened its eyes and growled softly. Reluctantly, Bernie Shepard reached into his pocket and removed a pair of glasses. When he had the glasses on, he looked around the roof and saw nothing. Still the dog growled. Shepard picked up the shotgun and took a step away from the shade of the water tower and into the moonlight. The dog was now on its feet, its head turning toward the chimney behind the tower.

"Too damn quiet," Shepard said softly to himself. "Just like an old war . . ."

A burst of static on the radio cut off the thought.

"Bernie," came Abe Lieberman's voice. "Bernie? We've got an emergency situation down here."

"And maybe one up here too," Shepard said, looking around.

He was alert, gun at the ready as Lieberman's voice went on, "Kearney's been shot. Some crackhead saw you on television. Came with a pawnshop special and tore into Kearney on the street. It doesn't look like Kearney will . . ."

The dog was growling softly and walking toward the concrete barricade. Shepard dropped the phone and spun around, shotgun up, aimed over the head of the dog into the darkness under the tower. Since there was no sound and no motion in the shadows, Shepard thought—but just for an instant—that the pain in his side was a shock of protest from his ulcer. But that instant passed and Shepard both saw the handle of the knife and knew. He fired as he went down, the shot going over the dog, splattering the concrete and shattering the water cooler. The dog, confused, looked at the fallen Shepard, whose glasses now dangled from one ear.

"Stop him, man," said Emiliano "El Perro" Del Sol, stepping over the barricade, second knife in his hand. "Stop him or you got dog meat for dinner."

The dog was poised to leap now. El Perro shifted the knife slightly in his hand, ready. Bernie Shepard forced himself to his knees, put his glasses back on, and looked at the shotgun just out of reach.

"Back off," Shepard said. The dog backed off reluctantly and moved to his side.

El Perro moved carefully, knife ready, and kicked the shotgun further out of Shepard's reach.

"You got hardware in your belt and your shoe," said El Perro. "Take it out slow and throw it easy, or you'll be reaching for a blade in your throat."

Shepard slowly, painfully removed the pistols from his belt and his boot and shoved them toward El Perro. The dog whimpered.

"Hey," said El Perro in a stage whisper, leaning forward as if they might be overheard, "you really do have fuckin' dynamite up here. You weren't just jivin' them, man."

Shepard didn't answer. He knelt, wincing in pain, and reached for the handle of the knife in his side.

"Wouldn't take that out if I was you," said El Perro, picking up one of the pistols and kicking the other well across the roof. "Might bleed to death."

Shepard blinked once, gave El Perro a grin, gritted his teeth, pulled out the knife with a small grunt, and shifted it to his palm.

"Now drop it," said El Perro, aiming the pistol.

Shepard, his face suddenly drenched in sweat, considered his chances as El Perro stepped forward quickly and kicked the knife from his hand.

The dog was pacing now. A howl of frustration came from deep inside him.

"You're one fuckin' macho cop, man," said El Perro with genuine admiration. "But you ain't no cop no more. You're like me. More like me now than you think. You dyin' or something?"

Still on his knees, Shepard pressed his palms on the open wound and looked up at Del Sol, who squatted to get a better look at Shepard's face and the damage.

"Hey, what you did, Shepard," he said. "To your old lady and that cop? I'd do the same. No shit. Any man with balls would do the same thing. You know what? Fuck those people out there. I took my shot at you. I got my pay. Now, I'm getting the hell out of here. They wanna finish you off, they can do it themselves. How you like that?"

Emiliano reached over, retrieved his first knife, and wiped its bloody blade on a dark handkerchief he whipped from his pocket.

"Here," he said, tossing the handkerchief to Shepard, who grabbed it before he hit the roof.

Shepard made a hissing sound and the dog stopped howling.

"I hope you make it, old man," said El Perro, backing into the shadows. "I hope you make it, tear out the heart of that asshole Kearney who whored your old lady."

Shepard could barely see him, but El Perro's voice came out of the darkness.

"I hope you blow up the whole fuckin' city."

El Perro dropped the pistol, flipped the razor-sharp knife in the air, caught it neatly without taking his eyes from Shepard, and slid the knife into the sheath at his side as he took three steps backward into the shadows and disappeared.

Something touched Shepard's side. His first impulse was to swat it away, punch it away from his pain. He caught his fist coming down, opened it and let his hand come to rest on the dog's head.

"He's gone," Shepard told the dog.

"Bernie?" came Lieberman's voice.

The radio lay about a dozen feet in front of him.

With the whimpering dog at his side, Shepard took off his glasses, gritted his teeth, and slowly, painfully pulled himself along the roof toward the shelter of the concrete barricade.

"Bernie?" came Lieberman's voice again.

The radio was a few feet away from him now. Shepard picked up the radio and pushed the switch.

"I'm still alive," said Shepard, trying to keep the ripping pain from his voice.

"I thought you might be," said Lieberman.

"It was worth the try, Lieberman," said Shepard. "I'd have done the same."

"Let's talk, Bernie."

"Not tonight," said Shepard. "I've got things to do. Tell Kearney we still have a date in less than three hours. If you find Del Sol, which I don't think you will, he'll tell you that I'm not bluffing about the explosives."

"Never thought you were, Bernie," said Lieberman.

"Pass it on to Hartz. Don't call again."

Shepard pushed the switch and watched the lights of the radio shimmer and fade. He placed the radio, sticky with his own blood, on the top of the barricade before he crawled through, flipped on a flashlight, and groped for a first-aid kit in the canvas bag. The bag was wet. The shattered water container had drenched it.

"The door," Shepard said, nodding toward the steel door. The dog didn't understand at first.

"There," Shepard repeated. "The door."

This time the dog understood but was reluctant to move.

"Now," said Shepard sharply, and the dog padded out to take its position.

Shepard lifted his shirt to reveal the bloody hole in his side. From the kit, he removed a large gauze pad, which he pressed hard against the wound, clenching his teeth to keep from making a sound. He hissed and, with one hand holding the pad to his side, pulled out a roll of surgical tape. He ripped off a piece of tape with his mouth and pressed it to the pad, taping the pad awkwardly against his flesh. Then, with both hands now free, he tore more tape to fix the pad firmly against his flesh. He willed himself not to pass out as he tore off strips of tape and pressed them to pad and flesh to keep the blood from seeping through.

"Three more hours," he said between his teeth. "Just give me three more hours."

William Hanrahan leaned against the wall of Jason Belding's living room. He and Alan Kearney had listened to Abe Lieberman's side of the conversation with Shepard, had heard the shotgun blast. Now they watched as Lieberman placed the radio on the table near the window and Chief Hartz burst into the room.

"What was that shooting?" he shouted. "Where's Del Sol?"

"He went up ten minutes ago," said Kearney. "Bernie did the shooting."

"How do you . . . ?"

"Emiliano didn't go up with a gun," said Lieberman.

"He didn't . . . ?" Hartz asked incredulously, moving to the window and looking out as if he expected El Perro to be lying in the street.

"Maybe," he said hopefully, "he took one of Shepard's guns and shot him."

"Bernie's alive," said Kearney. "And we have reason to believe that the roof is wired with explosives."

Hartz turned from the window. His uniform was looking a little shabby now. The shirt was wrinkled and his tie loose.

"Three hours," said Hartz, checking his watch. Without a trace of conviction, he turned to Alan Kearney and added, "You are not going up there, Kearney. With these two officers as my witness, I am telling you that you are not going up there."

Hartz looked from Hanrahan to Lieberman as Kearney let out a short, bitter laugh.

"I'm not? I don't go up there and Bernie Shepard blows the neighborhood into chicken shit. He dies some kind of screwy martyr or something, and I'm the bastard who survives even though I turned Olivia Shepard into a whore, the dirty cop who was afraid to face the wronged and righteous husband."

Hartz tried not to look at Hanrahan and Lieberman now as he tried for sympathy in his voice. "You're being hard on yourself. We'll get through that door, and . . ."

"And Bernie will blow the building," said Kearney.

"What else can we do?" asked Hartz reasonably.

"Let's have two Fourth of Julys," said Lieberman. "Clear the neighborhood, cut off Shepard's contact, and tell him to go ahead and press his button."

"Well . . ." said Hartz, doing his best to look as if he were seriously considering the suggestion.

"That the way you want it, Chief?" asked Kearney. "You want to give me a direct order not to go up there? Tell the papers and the TV people and sound like you mean it?"

Hartz was silent; Kearney looked at Lieberman, who

opened his mouth as the phone rang. Hanrahan moved to the phone and picked it up. The others stood silent, listening.

"Hanrahan," he said. "No. . . . No."

He hung up the phone and turned.

"Anxman," he said. "Channel Nine wants to talk to Captain Kearney. I said . . ."

"We heard," said Hartz impatiently. "You were right. Captain Kearney, I've already told you not to . . ."

Kearney was shaking his head. Wound up tight, he stepped toward Hartz, who didn't back away.

"This has all been the way Bernie Shepard wants it. Since he parked out there, walked into that building, and killed his wife and another police officer. He wants me up there. You want me up there. The mayor wants me up there. I'd guess almost every good citizen wants me to go up there. Shoot-out on the roof, good guy, bad guy. Which one am I, Chief? Who are you betting on, Chief?"

Lieberman stepped between the two men.

"Let's let the building blow," he said gently. "Something smaller, uglier can go up. A Seven-Eleven. All of this will be a confused memory in two years."

"That what you want to do, Chief?" asked Kearney.

Kearney and Hartz were almost eye to eye now. Hartz didn't reply.

"That's what I figured," said Kearney, stepping past the chief of police, going out the apartment door, and slamming it behind him.

Mayor Aaron Jameson and Ty Wheeler sat drinking coffee in the mayor's office. A cigar burned in the ashtray next to the mayor. The world did not know the mayor smoked. It was not just the heart attack he had suffered the year before but the image he knew he projected when he was photographed with a large cigar. The news flickered and hummed soothingly on the television set. The mayor had removed his shoes, and Wheeler considered whether His Honor should go through the waiting members of the press clean shaven or looking as if he had had a long, difficult day. Wheeler would decide that later when the drama on the rooftop was settled. Newspapers were piled on the desk and floor.

" . . . less than three and a half hours from now," came the soothing, confident voice of the television anchor. "Minutes ago, as you saw, Police Chief Hartz expressed his full confidence in Captain Alan Kearney, saying that he was sure Kearney would handle the situation properly. Kearney is the man who Shepard claims seduced his wife and is therefore indirectly responsible for the deaths of four people in the last twenty-four hours. Shepard, one of the most decorated officers in the Chicago . . ."

"Enough, enough," said the mayor. "Turn that shit off."

Wheeler reached over and turned off the television set.

"You'll turn it back on in a minute."

The mayor laughed.

"A morbid addiction. An act of masochism. Watching one's minor claim to history footnoted by an insane renegade cop. I'd go up there myself if I thought it would do any damn good."

"No, you wouldn't, Aaron."

The mayor lifted his left leg and rubbed his foot.

"No, I wouldn't," he said. "Not unless I was sure I'd make it down alive. But think of how this would translate into votes if I did talk that crazy son of a bitch down."

"I don't think about what we can't have," said Wheeler. "What we have is Kearney, and we've got to get him up there."

"And then?" asked the mayor, reaching for his cigar.

Wheeler allowed himself a long pregnant pause as he poured himself another cup of coffee.

"We pray," said Wheeler, reaching over to turn the television set back on.

On the street a block from what he now thought of as Shepard's Tower, Alan Kearney stood alone, looking at the moonlight that stretched across the rippling waves of Lake Michigan.

He pounded his fist angrily against the top of his car. Something behind him, possibly the sound of laughter, made him turn. In the shadowed walkway between two buildings across the street stood Emiliano Del Sol. Kearney watched him for a second or two and then El Perro turned and disappeared. The urge to follow him, the anger that surged through him, moved Kearney to take two steps toward the walkway. A sound of footsteps on the sidewalk behind him stopped him.

"Alan," said Carla Duvier. "We've got to talk. Now."

Abe Lieberman was tired. This fact he confided in William Hanrahan, who in turned confided that his head was throbbing.

The two men sat in Jason Belding's kitchen, drinking Jason Belding's Artesian water.

"You know what this is?" asked Lieberman, holding up his glass. "Seltzer for a buck a bottle. We used to get it delivered to our door by Joey Schoenberg, in siphon bottles, a dime a bottle plus a nickel deposit."

"The kind of bottle like they spray in people's faces in the movies," Hanrahan said.

"The kind," confirmed Lieberman. "You talk to the doctor about the pain?"

Hanrahan shrugged and shifted his weight.

"He says that's the way it is. May always have it. I've got pills. Consider the alternative, Rabbi."

"Consider the alternative," Lieberman conceded, holding his Artesian glass up in a toast.

They clinked glasses.

"You call Bess?"

"I called," said Lieberman. "The kids want to go to a mall tomorrow if this is over. I hate malls. They make my knees ache."

"I hate Disneyland and Disney World and all that stuff,"

said Hanrahan. "Iris says she wants to go. I've been thinking I want to go to New Mexico."

"You gonna go to Disney?"

"I'm gonna go," said Hanrahan looking at the almost empty glass in his hand. "You know, Abraham, the worst thing about not drinking is I can't stop thinking about drinking. Before, I just drank and didn't think about it. I had time for other things. You know what I mean?"

They were silent for a long time, listening to the refrigerator hum, expecting voices in the next room.

"Kearney's going up," said Hanrahan.

"He's going up," agreed Lieberman.

Bernard Shepard's eyes were closed, but the sweat probed under his lids, stung the corners, and pried him into consciousness. The carbine on his lap slid to the roof. He had replaced the shotgun with the lighter weapon when he realized that he could feel only the slightest sensation in his left hand. He coughed, reached for the cup of water he had poured earlier, took a drink, and coughed again. The cough ate into his side. He bit his lower lip, adjusted his glasses, turned on the flashlight, and looked at his watch.

There were still two hours to go.

He turned on his side and watched the dog lap at the spilled water. Shepard was vaguely aware that the bottom of his pants were wet. Blood, urine, the spilled water? It didn't matter. He started to close his eyes again and then, sensing something, he reached for the rifle and looked toward the end of the roof.

The two bounty hunters were walking toward him. The big one and the one with no shirt and the ice cream tattooed on his stomach.

Shepard pulled himself up, using the carbine as a crutch. Sensing something wrong, the dog looked around in confusion and saw nothing but Bernie Shepard raising the small rifle. Shepard fired at the first figure, the big man, who fell. Then the other dead man with the tattoo on his stomach stepped over his partner and advanced on the swaying Shepard. Shepard fired again.

As the tattooed man fell, yet another figure, Andy Beeton, a bloody Andy Beeton, stepped over both men and moved toward Shepard. The dog cowered behind Shepard as Shepard wiped his sweating brow.

Shepard fired a third time and Beeton went down.

Shepard squinted into the darkness. When no new apparition appeared, he tucked the rifle under his arm, reached into his shirt pocket, and came out with a plastic bottle of Tylenol and codeine. He had taken four pills after El Perro had left. Breathing hard, he took four more, swallowed, chewed, gulped, and gagged them down, trying to find saliva but finding only the taste of metal, the metal of Emiliano Del Sol's knife blade.

The dog kept its distance now and watched the man carefully, uncertain, knowing that the man now saw or sensed something the dog could not understand.

The man suddenly spun, rifle in hand, in the direction of the water tower. His face was moist and pale as Olivia Shepard, bloody, in a billowing nightgown, stepped out of the darkness over the fallen bodies.

"I haven't got time for bad dreams," he said.

Olivia paused a dozen feet in front of him.

"No time," he said, his finger closing on the trigger. "No time."

His finger would go no further. He couldn't fire.

"You're not there," he said as another figure stepped out of the darkness. Alan Kearney, his old partner, the cause of the hell he had gone through, stepped to Olivia's side, took her hand, turned her toward him, kissed her deeply, hungrily, his hands going under her gown.

"No," shouted Shepard. "No."

The dog ran to the steel door as Shepard fired, and fired and fired again until there was nothing left to fire with or to fire at.

And suddenly they were gone. Olivia, Kearney, Beeton, the bounty hunters. Shepard staggered to the spot where the ghosts had stood and fallen. He stood there silently for a few seconds and then moved to the edge of the roof and shouted into the night, "Kearney, no more games. You hear? No games. I want you. The real you. Look at your watch, you bastard. I want you in two hours. God, how I want you."

Two minutes before Shepard had fired at the first apparition, Alan Kearney and Carla Duvier had sat in Kearney's car, finishing a brief conversation. Carla had said, "Obviously, then, there's no real point in . . ." But Kearney was only half listening to her. His thoughts floated toward the roof behind them, and when he forced them back down he heard her say, " . . . our simply having our names, our lives turned into . . ."

The first shot cracked through the night. Kearney opened his car door.

"Alan, close that damned door and listen to me. What the hell do you think I am, some frontier woman, crippling myself over the dirty laundry while my man goes off with the posse?"

Kearney got out of the car and looked up and then down the street at Lieberman, who was moving toward him.

"Captain," said Lieberman. "I think it's time to clear our people out of the area."

"He's not going to blow anything up before he gets his shot at me," said Kearney as the second shot came.

He was aware of the opening of the car door and the clatter of Carla's shoes on the street, but he didn't turn toward her.

"There are levels of crazy," said Lieberman.

"I know what Bernie Shepard's going to do. I lived with him ten hours a day for six years."

"Alan," said Carla softly, reasonably. "If you turn your head, you'll see me standing here. I suggest you do it because it may be the last time you see me."

"I'll get back to . . . ," Lieberman began.

Another rifle shot from the roof stopped him. Kearney

turned to Carla and said, "Carla, you said good-bye to me when you got in the car. All you wanted was a way to blame it on me so you could walk away without blaming yourself."

"Bullshit," she said, moving toward him.

God, he thought, she is beautiful.

"Go talk it over with your father," he said.

Now the rifle shots came quickly, one after another. All three of the people in the street looked up, though there was nothing to be seen. When silence had returned, Carla spoke again, holding in her anger, bringing her voice down.

"I'll take that as a confession that what Shepard said about you and his wife is true."

"I guess you will," said Kearney. "You won't be the first today."

"Not much more to say," she said.

"Nothing more," Kearney added.

"Captain," said Lieberman. "I think it's . . ."

Kearney didn't wait to hear what *it* was. He strode past both of them toward Shepard's Tower as the voice of Bernie Shepard called through the night and the distant sound of traffic.

"Kearney, no more games. You hear? No games. I want you. The real you. Look at your watch, you bastard. I want you in two hours. God, how I want you."

When Bernie Shepard turned away from the edge of the roof, the ghosts had returned. Shepard stood looking, sweating, empty rifle in hand. Before him stood Kearney, Olivia, Beeton, Carl, and Dave. He blinked with stinging sweat and when he opened his eyes, there stood Kearney, Olivia, Lieberman, and vague figures he didn't quite recognize.

He blinked again and he was in Slivka's Tavern. Kearney, Olivia, Beeton, Lieberman, his wife, and the others were alive, laughing. A crude banner reading CONGRATULATIONS, CAPTAIN KEARNEY was strung across the bar, and Shepard saw himself leaning against the bar, drinking a beer, watching his wife and Kearney, who leaned close to

136

her, whispering. Shepard watched himself lean closer, straining to hear.

"I don't need a big-brother lecture, Alan," she says. "I need you."

"Who's lecturing, Livy?" says Kearney. "And besides, it's my party. I can lecture if I want to. All I said was Bernie deserves a chance. No, you deserve a chance."

"You're right," says Olivia. "It's not a lecture. It's a speech from a soap opera. I've done more than try, Alan. I've changed, but he hasn't. It's not just his age. It's . . ."

Somewhere a voice tries to break through as Shepard watches a figure hand him a bottle of beer and Andy Beeton moves through the crowd toward Olivia and Kearney.

"Great party," says the voice in a deep box.

Shepard watches himself push away from the bar and raise his bottle in the direction of Alan Kearney and Olivia.

"To Captain Kearney and his future," the Shepard of the past toasts.

And an echo answers, "Fraud."

10

Estelle Povelchek was in a hurry to finish cleaning the mayor's office. Normally, she took her time, even moved the desks and chairs to vacuum under them, but normally the mayor and his tall assistant were not in the office slumped in their chairs, looking like they were waiting for a bus. Estelle had been cleaning this office for more than thirty years. She had developed both pride and routine and, when it was required, patience.

"I'm getting sick of this office," said the mayor, who had long ago removed his tie and shoes. "Now, is that ironic or is it ironic? I spend my adult life trying to get this office and now I dread sitting here."

"Well, you may not have to occupy it much longer," said Wheeler, who had not yet removed shoes and tie, though both were far looser than they had been a few hours earlier.

"Estelle," said the mayor, sitting up and rubbing his face to wake it up, "are you going to vote for me if Shepard blows up the North Side?"

Estelle continued to work, wielding her spray bottle of Lemon Pledge, trying valiantly to overcome the odor of dead cigars.

"I vote for you," she said. "What do I care for the North Side? I live still Division Street."

"And what do you particularly like about my administration?" the mayor continued, opening his eyes wide in the hope that weariness would escape.

"You don't make as much a mess as the last mayor," she

said, shaking her head and spraying Pledge. "Sure, I vote for you."

"I somehow don't find that an encouraging voter sample," Wheeler said.

"You know the trouble with this job?" said the mayor, standing up. "Too damn many days and nights like this about too many damn problems you can't anticipate. Excuse my language, Estelle."

"Is all right," said Estelle, now rubbing with a torn towel where she had sprayed. The towel informed the world that Estelle was a Party Animal.

Wheeler reached for some coffee and glanced at his watch. He moved quickly to the television.

"Ten o'clock news. Pick your channel, Aaron."

"Four, that's my lucky number today," the mayor answered with more than a hint of irony.

Light and color popped on the screen and Janice Giles's face appeared.

"And," the mayor continued, "we are in luck. My favorite anchorwoman is on the job."

"Anchorperson," Wheeler corrected.

On the television, Janice Giles looked earnestly at the viewing public and said, "And so the city of Chicago stands helplessly by, as it has for almost twenty-two hours, while one man holds an entire neighborhood captive. Minutes ago shots were heard from the roof where Sergeant Bernard Shepard has barricaded himself as he, and the world, count the minutes till his demanded confrontation with the man he claims seduced his wife and drove him to this act of emotional despair. Captain Alan Kearney has refused to speak to the press, but Police Chief Hartz did issue a brief statement just minutes ago that echoes the statement released earlier this evening by the office of the mayor."

The face of Marvin Hartz, blue cap on his head, hair in place, exuding confidence, now appeared on the screen.

"The neighborhood," he said, "has been secured, and efforts are under way to resolve the situation without damage to property and without further human injury."

"And," said Janice Giles earnestly, "If these efforts fail? Will Captain Kearney go on the roof and face Bernie Shepard?"

"The police of this city will not give in to demands of people engaged in criminal activity. We've learned from our Jewish allies in Israel that one cannot give in to those who take hostages. Captain Kearney is a member of this department. I think that answers the question."

The mayor and Wheeler exchanged glances.

"Israel?" asked Mayor Jameson, turning to Ty Wheeler, "Israel? What is he trying to do, save the Jewish vote? Estelle, you think Kearney'll go up on that roof?"

"Man who did what he did?" she said, moving to clean the television screen. "I don't know. I'll tell you what I know if you want to hear it."

"We want to hear it," said the mayor. "Right, Ty?"

"We are focused on your every word," agreed Wheeler, loosening his tie a little further.

"If I did thing like Shepard's wife, my husband would do same as Shepard. Same, exact. This Kearney don't go up on roof, he better change his name to Pedro and take the next bus to El Paso."

"Vox populi," said Wheeler, toasting Estelle. "The people have spoken."

On the television an old man and old woman were being interviewed. It was daylight and the interviewer was Janice Giles. The old man spoke slowly, deliberately, using his hands.

"Wrong is wrong," he said. "I'm not saying it's right to go around shooting people, shooting people with a gun. It's wrong, but you can see from the man's face that he suffered. That other one, the one that did it with his wife . . ."

"You mean Captain Kearney?" Janice Giles asked.

"Kearney, yes," said the old man. "He should face his medicine and go up there. If he's a man, that's what he'll do. He'll do that."

"And you'd do that?" asked the old woman incredulously.

"I'm not saying this Shepard is Charles Bronson," the old man said patiently. "Did I say he was Charles Bronson or something? He killed a man and a woman. He's not Charles Bronson, for God's sake. He's a murderer."

"And you'd go up there?" asked the old woman.

"I'd do it," the old man said emphatically.

"Like so much . . . ," the old woman began, but a sharp bleep cut off her word. "What do you think? This is some cowboy movie or something? He killed three men and a woman, for God's sake. He's a murderer."

"Who denied it?" asked the old man, completely ignoring the camera and facing the old woman.

"I'm not saying he's Charles Bronson. Did I say he was Charles Bronson? If I did, I'm sorry. But if he doesn't do something, what kind of man is that?"

"Who's he talking about now," the mayor asked, "Shepard or Kearney? Hell, what's the difference?"

The mayor, still bare of foot, got up and turned the sound down on the television. Having accomplished that task, he moved toward the cabinet near his desk.

"A small drink would be in order now, I think. Estelle, would you be so good as to join us?"

"Is all right?" Estelle asked Wheeler.

"It's all right," said the mayor. "I'm still mayor. Besides, I need to keep the loyalty of my supporters."

Bernie Shepard swayed, blinking at the ghostly apparitions before him: Kearney, Olivia, Beeton. The dead danced with the living. Then Carla Duvier stepped out of the darkness, followed by Chief Hartz, who beamed, his right hand out, as he advanced on Kearney in the tavern of Bernie Shepard's memory.

Hertz shook Kearney's hand and put his arm around Olivia, almost allowing his fingers to touch her breasts.

"Kearney," Hartz said confidentially so that Shepard had to strain to hear, "I can only stay a minute, but I wanted to come by and personally wish you my best."

Then he turned to Olivia and said, "You must be very proud of your husband. You make a fine couple."

Olivia glanced at Shepard as Kearney said, "This is Olivia Shepard, Chief. Bernie Shepard's wife."

Kearney nodded in the direction of the swaying Shepard, who held up his beer bottle in a mock toast to the chief or the happy couple.

"I'm sorry," said Hartz. "I . . ."

"That's all right," said Olivia, backing away. Kearney took a step after her, but Andy Beeton intercepted Olivia and started to talk to her.

Carla Duvier moved past Shepard as if he weren't there, but Bernie put out his arm and said, "Chief Hartz just said my wife and your boyfriend make a fine couple. What do you think?"

"My opinion," said Carla, pushing Shepard's arm out of the way, "is that it's getting late and I've got to be at work early tomorrow."

"Ah," said Shepard. "Almost forgot. You gonna keep bringing home the bacon and gold when you and Al get married?"

"I plan to," she said with thinly disguised sarcasm. "Why, do you think a wife's place is in the home?"

"In the home," he said, toasting her and grinning maliciously. "In bed. In the kitchen. I'm just a good old-fashioned, well-fed male chauvinist pig."

"And your wife?" asked Carla, looking at Olivia and Andy Beeton, who were head-to-head. "What does that make her? Good night. And if you want to get an early start on a wedding present for me and Captain Kearney, we're registered at Marshall Fields."

Shepard swayed, afraid he would fall, and muttered as she moved toward Kearney, "Bitch."

He wasn't sure if he was talking about Carla, Olivia, or all women. He took a few steps through the crowd toward Beeton, whose back was to him as he spoke to Olivia. Shepard reached out with his left hand to touch Beeton, to turn him around, to say . . . he didn't know what. And

Beeton did turn, the bloody Beeton whose face had been blown apart, a face inches from Shepard's.

Bernie staggered back and fired his rifle as Beeton's ghost moved toward him.

"The hell with it," said the mayor. "Go on home and get some sleep. I'm going to sack out on the sofa for an hour or watch a movie."

"I'll do the same in my office," said Wheeler, standing.

Even with the volume almost off, the voice behind the screen rose so that they could suddenly hear a few words. Wheeler turned up the volume. The reporter, standing on a city street, was saying, ". . . why Shepard is firing, but police are now urging everyone, including news crews, to clear the area."

The mayor rose from his chair, took three barefooted strides to the television, and pulled the plug from the wall. The reporter on the screen eked out like a deflated balloon and the screen went blank except for a point of light which flickered and then disappeared.

"Christ," shouted the mayor. "We just sit here waiting for a goddamn miracle, and if we don't get the miracle, we start packing our things and looking for a new pasture. The hell with it. If we can't save this thing politically, as a last resort we can do the right thing. Get me Hartz on the phone. I'm going to tell him to clear everybody out including his own men and then get a helicopter up there and drop a goddamn bomb on Shepard."

The mayor hovered over Wheeler who sat back in his chair, weary, silent.

"Well," said Aaron Jameson, "aren't you gonna try to talk me out of it, tell me I'm tired and I should wait a little longer, let Kearney go up there and lose his life?"

"No," said Wheeler.

"Then make the call."

Wheeler knew the signs and was no fool. He picked up the phone.

"Damned Republicans'll probably clear the rubble," said

the mayor, "put up a park, and erect a statue of Shepard right in the goddamn middle of it."

Chief of Police Marvin Hartz was pacing the living room of Jason Belding's apartment when the mayor's call came. Bill Hanrahan had the honor of picking up the phone as Hartz stopped pacing and looked at him, his face red, his slightly open mouth betraying his fear. Captain Alton Brooks, his SWAT uniform neatly pressed in contrast to the chief's now wrinkled uniform, stood, feet apart, hands folded in front of him, watching from the window.

"It's the mayor," said Hanrahan, holding the phone toward the chief, who took it reluctantly.

Hanrahan moved across the room to at least create the illusion that the chief had some privacy.

"Yes, Mr. Mayor," Hartz said, looking at Hanrahan, who pretended to be searching for something amid the paper rubble on a chair in the corner. Brooks simply stood there looking as if he were waiting for an order he knew was about to come. "I know . . . I believe that Captain Kearney plans to go up on the . . . No, I told him, ordered him not to go."

Hartz dropped his voice and turned his back on Hanrahan, who now pretended to have found what he was looking for.

"I told him he was risking . . ."

Hanrahan gave up pretending, threw down the papers, and headed for the front door. Hartz spotted him, covered the mouthpiece of the phone, and hissed, "You stay right here."

Hanrahan stopped, considered leaving the room in spite of the order, and decided against it. Instead, he leaned against the wall and looked directly at Hartz as the latter returned to his conversation.

"We can alert the SWAT copter to go to the assault alternative," he said, looking at Brooks, who gave only the slightest of nods to indicate that he was ready. Then Hartz continued on the phone with, "But I thought . . . Yes, I'll

clear all remaining officers and media from the area. . . .
I . . . yes, I understand fully."

Hartz hung up the phone and muttered almost, but not
quite, to himself, "Yes, I understand whose ass is on the
line." And then to Hanrahan he said aloud, "Find Kearney.
Don't talk. Just find him. Tell him I want him here now."

Hanrahan pushed away from the wall, looked at Brooks,
and left the apartment.

"Captain," said Hartz, "clear all personnel from the area
except your men on the door and the assault team. But remember, if they stay, they're volunteers."

"They'll stay," said Brooks.

"If we do have to go to the bomb . . . is it small?" Hartz
asked.

"If Shepard has the place wired, it doesn't matter how
small the bomb is. The chain reaction will . . ."

"Just do what you have to do," Hartz said, putting on his
cap. "Do it."

On the stairway to the roof, Officers Howell and Spiza
were again in their shirtsleeves at the metal door. Both were
wearing dark work glasses. Spiza was working on the metal
hinges of the door with a pinpoint and relatively quiet
blowtorch when Kearney and Lieberman started up the
stairs. To Lieberman, the two men looked like a formidable
tag team, one black, one white, both powerful.

Spiza didn't see them coming, but Howell did and
touched his partner's shoulder. Spiza turned off the torch
and lifted his glasses.

"How's it coming?" asked Kearney.

Howell tilted his glasses back and said, "Few minutes.
Good hit would probably take it down now."

Kearney looked back at the SWAT officer, who now
stood, rifle ready, at the foot of the stairs.

"He's out of control up there, you ask me, Captain," said
Spiza, looking at Howell for confirmation. Howell nodded.
"He's talkin' to himself," Spiza continued, "shooting. You
think he really has the place wired?"

"Yeah," said Kearney. "It's wired."

A radio crackled at the bottom of the steps and Lieberman was aware of the SWAT man's whisper.

"Chief Hartz is looking for you, Captain," called the SWAT man. "Wants you back at command fast."

"You haven't seen me," said Kearney without looking down.

"But . . . ," the SWAT man began, only to be cut off by Kearney's taking three steps up and throwing his shoulder at the steel door, which screeched and started to give way.

Both Spiza and Howell had moved out of Kearney's way, but Lieberman came after him.

"Holy shit," cried the SWAT man, lifting his rifle and dropping the phone.

"Captain," Lieberman said, grabbing Kearney's arm.

"Back off," said Kearney with a touch of madness in his face and words. "Back off and clear out. All of you, fast."

"Captain," the SWAT man shouted. "The chief says he does not, repeat, does not want you to go up there."

"I think they changed their minds in City Hall, Captain," said Lieberman softly as Howell and Spiza inched down a step or two.

"It doesn't matter," said Kearney. "I'm going out there."

"Then," said Lieberman with a sigh, "we're going out there, but remember I've got a wife, a daughter, and two grandchildren, and tickets to Sunday's doubleheader."

"I'll bear that in mind," said Kearney.

Alton Brooks stood in the street, looking up and listening to his radio. He watched as two of his men came out of a top-story window of the Shoreham. They were dressed completely in black. Even the rifles slung over their backs were black.

One of the men raised a hand and waved down. Brooks waved back and the men began to search for footholds and places to grip for their climb to the roof.

"Captain Kearney passed Station Two at . . . ," the voice on the radio had said, only to be cut off by another voice adding, "Captain Kearney's here at Station Three. I gave him the order. He ignored me. He's opening the door, Zebra One, please advise."

"Hit the lights, Briggs," said Brooks clearly, quickly, decisively to his man at the main switches in the Shoreham basement.

On the roof of the Shoreham, Bernie Shepard turned toward the sound of screeching metal as the door began to open inward. Shepard wiped the sweat from his eyes and adjusted his glasses as Kearney stepped forward with someone behind him. Shepard watched the dog move toward the apparition, and Kearney reached down to pat its head.

Shepard wasn't sure whether it was really Kearney or another ghost. He looked toward the open hole where the door had been and saw only darkness.

"Get away from him," Shepard called to the dog as he raised his weapon. "It's too soon." He faced Kearney and checked his watch saying, "You've got another hour."

"I'm calling this one, Bernie," Kearney said, stepping forward. "Hartz just ordered me out of the area. I don't think he gives a shit if you blow up half the North Side. You let it go on too long, Bernie. You let it go on too long to get back at me. Now no one cares about you, this building, the entire North Side. Hartz wants you dead."

Shepard laughed and looked at Lieberman and then back at Kearney.

"Christ, you're not real, either of you. But you will be in an hour. The real you will come up here. I can wait another hour. I can wait forever if I have to. Get out."

Shepard raised his rifle quickly and took aim as Kearney stepped toward him.

"Shepard," said Lieberman. "I'm not a ghost. I'm a very worried cop with about a dozen other worried cops in this building."

"You been seeing ghosts, Bernie?" asked Kearney. "Well, I'm no goddamn ghost either. Not yet."

Shepard cocked his head warily to one side to study the

two men before him. Then he smiled, a slow smile that turned into another laugh.

"You couldn't wait," he said. "You couldn't wait, so you came an hour early. And that is fine. You know why it's fine? Because I lied a minute ago, Al. I can't wait forever. I might not even make it another hour. I'm up to my ass in blood here and some of it's mine. Believe in destiny, Al, 'cause that's what brought you up here."

Shepard pulled up his shirt. The bandage in the light of the moon was black with blood.

"You sent the copter," said Shepard. "The two clowns, the Mex, but they couldn't stop this from happening, Kearney. You wasted your time."

"Shepard," said Lieberman reasonably. "You put down the gun. We walk down those stairs. You get a public trial where you can tell everyone in the world your story. And no one else dies."

"Sounds reasonable," said Shepard. "But that's a whimper instead of a bang. I'm going out with a bang. Abraham, get your kosher ass out of here if you're so goddamn concerned about your family."

"Bernie," said Kearney. "You're a goddamn fool."

"I'm a . . . ? And what's your day been like, Captain? Is there anything left of your life? Is that why you came running up here early? God, I'm going to enjoy killing you."

"Bernie, you are one fucking hypocrite."

"I'm a . . ."

Shepard raised his rifle and fired into the night inches over Kearney's head.

"You screw your partner's wife, turn her into a whore, and I'm a . . ."

". . . fool," Kearney continued, now only half a dozen feet from Shepard. "She did what she did because you're a cold, self-righteous, unbending asshole. You treated her the way you treated everyone else, by the book. You weren't a husband. You were a keeper. You never listened to her, me, anyone in your life."

Spiza, Howell, and the SWAT cop hovered back in the

darkness of the stairwell next to the steel door that hung broken on a single twisted hinge. They had their weapons ready. They strained to hear the conversation on the roof but could catch nothing and could see little beyond the back of Sergeant Lieberman, who blocked most of their view.

The two SWAT men scaling the side of the building now reached the tiled eaves of the roof.

In Jason Belding's apartment fifteen stories below, Captain Alton Brooks stood, hands at his side, watching.

On the roof Bernie Shepard, swaying feverishly now, held the rifle aimed at Kearney's stomach.

"You are a lying bastard," said Shepard.

It was Kearney's turn to laugh.

"Lying? What the hell have I got to lie about? I know you, Bernie. I'm not trying to change your mind. No one can do that. I just want you to know how much you fucked up. You think I screwed around with Livy?"

"I know you did, you shit. I watched you. You were my partner. I followed her to your place Thursday night. I waited. Three hours I waited. And when I went home later and asked where she'd been, she lied."

Kearney shook his head.

"You asshole," he said. "I was her friend. Friend. Do you know what that is? No, you don't. I should know that idea wouldn't get through to you. All you can think of between men and women is who's on top and how long. I could have taken her. When she cried and complained about what a frozen bastard you are. I could have taken her. I told her you wouldn't change. She thought she could change you when you were married. I warned her, told her what you were, said you were too old and too damn mean to change, but she saw something in you. She was wrong."

"Beeton," Shepard shouted. "The others."

"Who the hell knows, Bernie?" Kearney shouted back. "Maybe she wanted you to catch her. Maybe she was looking for a cop who'd treat her like a person. Shit, maybe she was looking for some simple sex. I'm not excusing her. She

149

doesn't need any excuses. You didn't give her a chance to give one. She's dead. No one betrayed you, Bernie. No one but Bernie Shepard."

Shepard looked at Kearney and blinked his eyes. Confused, he raised his rifle toward the tower where he had placed the detonator. It was clearly marked with a spot of yellow glowing paint and he was reasonably sure that, even in his condition, he could still hit it from thirty feet.

"Shit," muttered Lieberman. "Shepard, don't . . ."

"Lying," said Shepard, blinking his eyes clear so he could keep the yellow spot in focus. "You're a lying son of a bitch trying to save your dirty pimping skin."

"I'm not lying and you know it," said Kearney. "What I'm telling you doesn't bring Livy or Beeton or those two assholes you shot back. It won't even save you and it sure as hell isn't helping me any. It doesn't do anything but show you that this whole self-righteous pile of shit was a stupid waste."

"No," shouted Shepard, his sweating forehead beet red with strain. "Self-respect. There's nothing else. In the end it's just lies and bad dreams if you don't respect yourself."

Shepard tried to hold aim on the yellow dot. He moaned softly in anger and frustration, and wiped the moisture from his glasses and forehead with his sleeve. Somewhere behind him the dog groaned in confusion. Shepard's finger tightened on the trigger, and Lieberman had an instant to wonder if the look on Shepard's face showed any understanding of the horror of what he had done.

And then suddenly Bernie Shepard's face went slack—not, Lieberman decided, from pain, but resignation. There seemed to be a spark of terrible comprehension in his eyes as he lowered the rifle.

Shepard opened his mouth to speak, and to Lieberman there was something strange and mystical about the sweating man. For an instant Lieberman did not understand the pinpoint of red light on Shepard's forehead, a mark like the sign of Cain. Then he knew that Kearney had recognized the spot.

The dog was now running toward the doorway.

"No," shouted Kearney, turning toward the open door where he sensed but couldn't see the SWAT man in the stairwell.

The dog leaped into the darkness and the SWAT man held up his rifle to keep the snarling animal from his throat.

A rifle shot.

For a beat both Lieberman and Kearney were confused and then they saw, beyond the back of Bernie Shepard, at the edge of the roof, two dark shadows.

Shepard dropped the rifle and fell in dying pain to the sound of dog and man battling in the darkness. As he slumped to the roof, Shepard's glasses fell from his face. He reached for them a good foot from where they clattered to the stones.

Kearney and Lieberman moved to Shepard, who held out his hand. Kearney reached for it, but the hand went limp. Bernie Shepard was dead.

The two SWAT men advanced toward the body as dog and SWAT man fell onto the roof through the doorway.

"Stop," shouted Kearney at dog and man.

The dog stopped first.

The bloody SWAT man stepped back and aimed at the animal.

"I said stop," Kearney shouted again, and the man lowered his weapon.

The dog smelled, sensed something now. It turned its head toward the two shadows holding black rifles and ran to Shepard's body. The men on the roof stood watching as the dog looked to each of them for an answer and then began to howl at the full moon.

Kearney turned his back on the scene and went past the broken steel door. The dog made a decision. It looked at Lieberman and trotted after Kearney into the darkness of the stairway.

The street was filled with people. There had been the

sounds of the dog, a single shot, no explosion, and then the horrible howling.

Hartz and Brooks looked at the Shoreham from the doorway of the building where the command post would no longer be needed.

A television crew struggled to get past four police officers at the end of the street. Radios crackled and the voice of a SWAT man came through the night with, ". . . secured. I repeat, secured. Subject is down . . ."

Hartz spotted Kearney coming through the front door of the Shoreham with the dog at his side. He started toward him, but Kearney moved through the crowd, heading into the alleyway next to the building where he had reparked his car.

Hartz hurried toward him through the crowd as another voice on the radio said, ". . . need aid for Tolliver. Medic, ambulance. Advise bomb squad. It is wired and hot."

"What happened?" Hartz demanded.

Kearney ignored him and opened the door of his car.

"Captain Kearney," Hartz shouted. "What the hell happened?"

Kearney closed the door and without looking back drove a dozen feet, stopped suddenly, and reached back to open the rear door. The dog ran past Hartz and leaped in. The door closed and Chief Hartz found himself standing alone and without his answer as the car groaned off into the night.

11

It was just after three in the morning when William Hanrahan parked in front of his house in the Ravenswood section of Chicago. Ravenswood, sandwiched between the decay to its south and the terrors of Uptown to the north, almost held its own thanks to the stubborn old-timers like Hanrahan and the young blue collars who wanted some stability but could not afford a suburb.

Parking was never a problem on Hanrahan's street. There was only one apartment building on either side of the street. The rest of the block was small houses with little front yards. Ravenswood Hospital was two blocks away, just far enough so visitors and staff who couldn't get into the parking lot wouldn't be tempted to stray this far.

Hanrahan needed a drink. He sat in the car looking at the night breeze fluttering the branch of a tree in front of the streetlight. No, he corrected himself, he did not need a drink. He wanted one and he knew where to find it, the one Beer of Temptation he kept in the back of the refrigerator. He had convinced himself that if he could resist the urge of that beer, the lies his devious mind created for taking it, if he could resist that single beer, he could resist anything. But, God, it was only a beer. And nothing, nothing tasted like a beer. Iced tea, Coke, coffee—nothing satisfied Hanrahan's thirst. It wasn't as if he wanted a double J&B from Sandy's.

Hanrahan looked at himself in the mirror over the dash.

"What do you see?" he asked softly. "I'll tell you what you see. You see a man lying to himself is what you see."

Hanrahan opened his door, shifted his weight, and stood up in the street. Far away, probably on Wilson, cars swished by. The breeze rustled the trees on the dark street, and Hanrahan closed his door.

A twinge over his right eye reminded Hanrahan of his healing wound and gave him another hint for an excuse. The pain. Bernie Shepard's death. The memory of Olivia Shepard and Andy Beeton in the bedroom. Maureen's leaving him. His sons' blame. Hell, there was a world of reasons out there to have a drink.

He walked to the sidewalk, pushed open the low wrought-iron gate, and went up to the door. Hard to tell, but it looked like the paint on the wood trim was fading. He would work on that this weekend. Maybe he would paint the whole porch. No, he had promised Iris Huang that he would drive her up to Antioch to pick up some dishes or something for the Black Moon Restaurant. Sunday then. He would do it Sunday if it didn't rain.

God, he thought as he opened his front door and went in, he was thirsty. It would be impossible to sleep and he had to get in before eleven in the morning to work with Lieberman on their report. The hell with it, he decided. Who knows? Who cares? One beer to help me sleep. After what I've been through.

He stepped toward the kitchen, knowing the way without seeing, and heard the sound. A creak, a footstep. Someone was standing on the stairs leading up to the bedrooms.

Most of the houses on the block had been broken into in the last few years. Until now, Bill Hanrahan's house had escaped. Hanrahan dropped to one knee in the shadow near the living room and pulled out his gun, knowing that whoever was there had already adjusted to the darkness.

"Freeze," Hanrahan said.

The figure on the stairs shifted and caught its breath.

"It's me," said a thin voice.

Hanrahan reached up, hit the wall switch while keeping his weapon leveled on the steps.

Jeanine Kraylaw looked at the gun with wide eyes.

"He's here?" she said, looking around desperately. "Frankie is here?"

She wore an extralarge T-shirt with the words UNGRATE-FUL DEAD printed in red block letters. Her long brown-blond hair fell over her face. Her dark eyes scanned the small alcove.

"No," said Hanrahan, putting the pistol away and standing. "I . . . I forgot you were here."

"Oh," she said. "I'm sorry."

"You can go back to bed," he said, feeling a slight ache in his knee where he had knelt. He never knelt on the knee when he had time to think. There was a metal pin in there, had been for more than twenty-five years. It had ended his football dreams.

"You just gettin' in?" she asked.

"Yeah," he said.

He could see her breasts pushing out the first U and the last D in UNGRATEFUL DEAD.

"I'm gonna have a glass of water and get some sleep myself," he said, walking to the kitchen.

She padded in barefoot behind him as he turned on the kitchen light and moved to the refrigerator. He got his bottle of water out, went to the cabinet, poured two glasses, and went to the table. He hadn't looked at the green bottle in the back of the refrigerator.

Jeanine was sitting, her arms folded over her breasts as if she were chilled. He handed her a glass and she took it with a "Thank you."

Hanrahan sat and they drank their water silently. Jeanine had to brush her hair back with her hand once or twice.

"Good water," she said.

"Thanks."

Silence again.

"I don't know what Charlie and I are gonna do," she said finally. "I mean, I'm not complainin' or askin' you for anything. I'm just . . . you know, talkin'. We made a few eggs and stuff."

"That's fine. You can take what you want. How old are you, Jeanine?" Hanrahan asked.

"Twenty-four," she said. "Can I say somethin'?"

"You can say something," he said.

"I'm scared. Not so much of Frankie. You know what I'm talkin' about?"

"I think so."

"Good, 'cause I ain't so sure."

More silence. Hanrahan felt his eyes close. He snapped them open and started to get up. Jeanine beat him to it and swept up both empty glasses. Hanrahan didn't try to stop her.

"I put Charlie in the bedroom over in the corner like you said," she said, moving to the sink.

"It was my sons' room," he said.

"You have a son?"

"Two. They're grown now. Live in other cities. The one in Buffalo, Mike, that's the one I'm gonna call about getting you some work. I think you should get out of this town soon and far."

"You do think Frankie's coming back," she said.

"I think the fewer risks you take, the longer you're likely to live."

She turned from the sink and looked at him.

"Your wife? She keeps a nice house. Where . . . ?"

"Left me about four years ago. I think I'll get some sleep now. Just turn out the lights when you come upstairs."

He rose.

"You want me to sleep with you?" she said suddenly, quickly.

Hanrahan was almost to the door. He turned and looked at her frightened face.

"Jeanine, you don't have to pay your way like that. We'll get you a job, and if you want to, you can pay me a few dollars when you're all set up."

"No," she said. "I'm scared to be alone. Maybe that's why I didn't leave Frankie before."

Hanrahan laughed. "No," he said. "I'm not laughing at you."

"Then why're you laughin'?"

"There's an old Irish story," he said. "Paddy and Mike are walking down the street, and Paddy suddenly stops and says, 'Did you hear that?' 'What?' asks Mike. 'That terrible noise,' says Paddy. 'No,' says Mike. 'It's as I thought, Michael,' says Paddy. 'I'm going crazy.' 'Thank the Lord,' says Mike. 'For a minute I thought I was going deaf.' "

Jeanine looked at him puzzled.

"Are you Irish?" she asked.

"That I am," he said, wiping tears of laughter from his eyes.

She shook her head.

"My bedroom's the one to the right upstairs," he said.

"I know."

He held the kitchen door open for her.

"You go climb in my bed. The sheets are clean. There's an old sofa in the room. I'll sleep on it so you won't be alone, but I've got to brush my teeth and shower. In the morning, we'll see how Abe is doing getting you some work. Okay?"

"Okay," she agreed, moving past him into the hallway.

"I snore," he warned.

"Worse than that been keepin' me up. I can tell you."

"Tomorrow I'll make you and the boy an Irish breakfast just like my mother used to make me."

"What's that?"

"Fried egg foo young." Hanrahan laughed again. "I'm not crazy," he said. "Just up too late. Get some sleep, little lady."

"Thank you," she said, and padded into the hall and up the stairs.

Hanrahan looked around the kitchen, decided that everything was in place. He had kept the house like this in the hope and fear that Maureen would one day knock at the door. He would let her in and she would see without his having to say it that he was doing very well on his own, that he didn't need her. It was never quite clear to him whether his ultimate purpose was to get her back, to hope that she had heard that he was now sober and responsible, or simply to imagine himself rejecting her, saying that he was going on with his life.

He thought of Bernie Shepard again. He saw Shepard and his wife, a fleeting pair of ghosts in the dark corner of his living room, whispering. He knew they weren't there, that his mind was telling him something, that the faint outline was only the flower pattern of the chair and lamp in the corner.

Bill Hanrahan went upstairs to sleep on his couch.

Frankie Kraylaw stretched his legs when the bus stopped in Effingham, Illinois. It was a little after one in the morning. Most of the people on the bus got out for coffee, a smoke, a clean toilet, or a sandwich. When the lights had gone off on the bus about two hours earlier just outside of Chicago, some guy with a foreign accent had started to moan in the dark. "I got no friends. I got no family."

People had answered, even laughed.

"Hey man. You better off."

"You think you got a sad story? I'll tell you a real one."

"Shut the fuck up, man. I wanna sleep."

Frankie tried to find the voice in the dark. He wanted to sit near him, tell him that God was his friend and family, that he, Frankie Kraylaw, knew what it was like to have your family taken from you. It had just happened to Frankie, but God had told him to start thinking about going back. You can't just walk away from your responsibilities. That's what Frankie would tell him.

"Oh, shit," hissed the gray-haired black man next to Frankie at the window. "Driver, shut that son of a bitch up."

"No friends. No family. No love," moaned the man with the foreign voice.

"The man is crying for help." said Frankie softly to the black man.

"I got me an ulcer. I got me a bad heart. I got no work and my only sister is dyin' in Memphis," said the black man. "I paid my ticket and I need my sleep. I don't need no feel-sorry-for-himself Russian or whatever, and I sure as fuck in the mornin' don't need no half-wit white kid like you tellin' me what's what or who's who or why's why. So just leave me be."

Frankie grinned knowingly in the dark. The rage was in him. The rage that the Lord sent through him when someone failed to see, to understand the sanctity of marriage, of family.

They were at the bus stop now, and Frankie stood just outside the bus, waiting for the old black man to come, hoping the lonely man with the foreign accent would get off and do something to let Frankie recognize him.

Frankie was feeling better now. He had a mission. He would complete his mission and then, in spite of the big Irish cop and the little Jew who knew nothing of the salvation of the Lord, he would return to his family.

Lieberman walked around to the rear of the house so he wouldn't disturb Barry and Melisa sleeping in the living room. A few nights earlier he had tripped over Barry in the late night darkness, not knowing that his grandson had moved his bedroll near the door.

So Abe went through the yard, opened the screen door as quietly as he could. Bess had left the small porch light on, thank God. He opened the door, pushed it open slowly, carefully, gently, and went into the kitchen.

The twenty-watt night-light over the stove was on. Lieberman closed the door gently, moved to the door of the living room, closed it, and turned on the kitchen light.

There was a note on the table and a can of Coke. Lieberman read the note:

Abe,
Maish dropped by with soup, pickled fish, kishke, and

some fresh rolls. Eat what you like, but remember don't use the microwave. Lisa wants to talk to you in the morning.

Love, Bess

Lieberman went to the refrigerator, took out the whitefish and a bottle of caffeine-free Diet Coke, and went back to the table, trying to decide whether it was worth going to bed for an hour or two or just waiting till the sun came up.

The Coke can on the table was wearing glasses. It had a little black button on top where the tab should have been. Abe took a bite of whitefish and pushed the button.

A voice crackled through the room with the name, "Sergeant Bernard Shepard."

Lieberman, forkful of whitefish almost to his mouth, stared at the Coke can, which crinkled and danced to the voice of an early morning news report on WBBM.

". . . shot at least seven times by . . ."

Lieberman pulled himself together, reached over, and turned off the Coke-can radio. The can crinkled back into shape.

"It's Barry's," Lisa whispered from the kitchen doorway. "He thought you'd find it funny."

"I cannot tell you how amused I am," Lieberman told his daughter as she closed the kitchen door gently.

He watched her warily as he returned to his whitefish plate and opened the half-full bottle of Diet Coke. She moved to the table and sat across from him. She was wearing a blue terry-cloth robe, and he remembered how she had liked a purple terry-cloth robe of his when she was three or four years old. She had called it his towel robe.

Now she sat silently across from him, watching him eat.

"We saw about Sergeant Shepard on the news," she said. "Mom was worried."

"Worried?"

"You were up on the roof. Guns, explosives. Why are you incredulous?"

"I don't know," he said. "Lack of sleep. Inherent stupidity. I'll talk to her."

"Take her on vacation," said Lisa.

"I thought your degree was in biochemistry, not family counseling," he said.

"Is that a comment on how I've managed my marriage?" she asked without rancor.

Lieberman looked up from his food. Lisa should have been seething by now.

"No," he said.

"You talked to Todd today."

"Yesterday," he said. "It's already tomorrow."

"You think I'm wrong," she said.

"About . . . ?"

"Leaving Todd," she concluded.

"Who knows? I don't have to live with him. I think he's a decent man. I think he loves you and the kids. I think he doesn't know what you want. I also think, if we're being honest here, that he can drive someone nuts. He's as depressive as those Greeks he can't stop quoting. So who knows?"

"Be honest about me," she said.

Lieberman looked at his daughter and sighed. It was almost four in the morning, about the time he usually woke up knowing that he would get no more sleep, unwilling to leave Bess and the bed in the hope that sleep might come. He was in the gray dawn area of mistakes one regrets.

"You're my daughter. I find you very difficult."

"That's it?" she asked softly, hurt.

Abe looked at his fizzing glass of Diet Coke and then at the Coke can with glasses.

"I love you. I don't think walking away from your husband with two kids is going to make you happy, but who knows? I don't know if anyone is supposed to be happy. People go around looking for happy and not finding it when they should be looking for content."

" 'Hope for the best. Expect the worst,' " she said. "Mel Brooks."

"A variation on my philosophy at four in the morning after a very tough night," he explained.

"Are you happy, Dad?"

"I am. . . . There are deep holes and high notes," he said. "I'm not unhappy."

Lisa got up.

" 'The unrighteous are never really fortunate. Our hopes for safety depend upon our doing right,' " she said. "Euripides. *Helen*, act one. He has me doing it."

"Use *Euripides* in a sentence," he asked.

She shrugged.

"Euripides pants. I breaka you neck," he said flatly without a hint of humor.

"Thanks, Dad," she said with a groan. "I'm going back to bed."

"You're welcome," said Lieberman. "I don't know what I said, but I'm glad it helped."

She came around the table, leaned over, and kissed his forehead.

Ten minutes later Lieberman had shaved, showered, changed into his robe, and tiptoed to his and Bess's room. He opened the door gently and closed it, making his way to the bed and placing his pistol in the drawer, which he locked with the key he wore around his neck.

And then he climbed into bed.

"Lieberman," said Bess in the dark.

"I woke you," he said.

"I wanted to be wakened. I thought it would be nice to know that you were still alive. What time is it?"

"A little after four. I'm still alive," he said.

They said nothing for a minute or two.

"How was your meeting?" he asked.

"Ida Katzman and Rabbi Wass want you back on the building committee," she said. "So does the president of Temple Mir Shavot, which is me."

"Rabbi Wass wants me back on the building committee because Ida Katzman wants me on the committee. Rabbi Wass thinks I am an atheist."

"He doesn't know you like I do."

"Do you think I'm an atheist?"

"Who knows?" she said. "I think you need some sleep."

"I think I need a vacation."

"Sounds good to me," said Bess. "Wednesday we're taking Barry and Melisa to the zoo. Can you make it?"

"There's a boy about Barry's age and a young woman staying a few days with Bill Hanrahan. Maybe they can come with?"

"Why not?" said Bess. "Abraham?"

"Yes."

"It's all right," said Bess.

And without knowing what she meant, he understood and wept.

LIEBERMAN'S DAY
Stuart M. Kaminsky

is now available in bookstores!

Published in hardcover by Henry Holt
and Company.

Read on for the first chapter of
LIEBERMAN'S DAY. . . .

Two Minutes Past Midnight
on a Winter's Night
in Chicago

Cold.

The frozen-fingered wind goes mad and howls, beating the lid of the overflowing green dumpster in a metal-against-metal tattoo. Ba-bom, *boom*-boom.

Through the narrow slit between the concrete of the two high-rise buildings, Lake Michigan, not quite frozen at the shore, throws dirty ice chunks onto the narrow beach and retreats with a warning roar.

"It is cold, man. I tell you. I don't care what you say. I don't care how you say. It is cold."

George DuPelee, his huge body shivering, his shiny black face contorted and taut, shifted from booted foot to booted foot. George wore a knit hat pulled down over his ears and an oversized olive drab military overcoat draped down to his ankles. He was hugging himself with unmatched wool gloves, one red and white, the other solid purple.

Boom-boom.

George grabbed the frigid rusting metal of the dumpster lid and pushed it down on the frozen plastic sacks of garbage inside it. The angry wind rattled the lid in his hand and it broke free. Boom-boom-boom-boom.

"What are you doing?" Raymond whispered irritably, adjusting his glasses.

"Goddamn noise driving me nuts," George whispered back. "I don't like none of this none. I don't like this cold."

George certainly looked cold to Raymond Carrou, who stood beside him in the nook behind the massive garbage cans. Raymond was lean, not an ounce of fat to protect him under his Eddie Bauer jacket, and he, too, was cold; not as cold as George DuPelee, but cold.

It was December in Chicago. It was supposed to be cold. People like George and Raymond didn't come here from Trinidad to enjoy the warm days and cool nights. People came to the States to make a dollar or to get away from something.

George DuPelee was a complainer. Raymond had known George for only a few days and he was now deciding that, however this business turned out, after tonight he would deal no more with the whining giant whose teeth rattled loudly as the two men waited for an acceptable victim to come out of the apartment building.

By the dim light of the mist-shrouded streetlamp, George watched the cars no more than twenty yards away on Sheridan Road lug through the slush, sending sprays of filthy ice over the sidewalk. Sheridan Road at this point north of Lawrence was a canyon of high-rise condominiums through which the wind yowled at the cars that passed through on the way to Evanston going north or downtown going south.

"Tell me you ain't cold," George challenged. "Tell me. Skinny thing like you. Got no fat. Wind go through your bones and you no more used of this than me." George concluded with a grunt of limited satisfaction, pulling his hat more tightly over his ears and continuing his steady foot-to-foot shuffle.

"Cold never bothered me much," said Raymond, watching as the door to the building opened and an old couple came out already leaning into the night as the blast of icy air ran frozen across their faces and down their backs.

"Them, they old, rich, no trouble, no bubble," said George, his bulky body nudging Raymond toward the light beyond the shadows of the buildings and the dumpster.

Raymond watched the old couple struggle against the cold wind. The old man almost toppled over, but caught his balance just in time and moved cautiously forward, gasping through the wind, reaching behind him to pull the old woman with him.

"No," said Raymond, stepping back into the shadow so the old couple wouldn't see him.

"No," moaned George, turning completely around in a circle like a frustrated child. "No. Man, what we come all the way down here for? Places closer. Over back there on Chestnut, you know? Look at those old olds. They got money, rings, stuff. Just take it, throw them old people in the air and let the wind take them."

"Up," said Raymond, his eyes back on the entrance to the high-rise condo building.

"Up?"

"Up," said Raymond. "We came uptown, north, not downtown."

George stopped turning and looked as if he was going to cry.

"Up, down, what's the difference here? I got no watch. I got no need. I got no job like you got."

Raymond ignored him and looked up one-two-three-four-five-six floors to a lighted window covered with frost. A shape, a woman, stood in the window.

"Carol?"

Carol turned away from the window and faced Charlotte Flynn.

"Carol, are you all right?" Charlotte said. "You look . . ."

"Fine," said Carol, touching the older woman's hand and giving her a small, pained smile. "Just tired."

"God," said Charlotte looking at her watch. "I . . . It's past midnight. Poor thing. You must be exhausted."

Carol shrugged.

Charlotte was a sleek, elegant woman in a simple black dress. Charlotte was plastic-surgery taut with a cap of perfect silver hair. Charlotte had been the wife of a television station manager for more years than Carol had been on earth. And Charlotte's husband was, for another month, the boss of Carol's husband, David. In one month, David was being transferred by the network to New York City where he would be program manager. Not exactly higher in rank or salary than Bernie Flynn, the jobs were not parallel, but certainly equal to Bernie with the promise, no, the likelihood, that David would one day be Bernie's boss if Bernie did not retire or move on.

And so, the evening had been, as Carol knew it would be, awkward. Awkward and long. Carol wondered at least five times, through poached salmon she could barely touch and conversation that had an edge sharp enough to cut a throat, whether she could keep from screaming.

"I think David should get you home." Charlotte said gently, taking Carol's hand. "Your hands are freezing."

"Circulation," said Carol. "Doctor says it's normal."

"I don't remember," Charlotte said. "My last, youngest, Megan, is thirty-four. I have a vague sense of being pregnant for two or three years and suffering two hours of something white and loud that must have been pain."

Carol nodded.

"Oh, God," Charlotte said, closing her eyes and shaking her head. "That was a stupid thing for me to say."

"It's all right," Carol said. "Really. I think we should go."

"Sit down," Charlotte said. "I'll get David and your coat."

The older woman strode confidently through the thick-gray-carpeted living room/dining room furnished in contemporary Scandinavian white wood, the look broken up only by the out-of-place yet tasteful eighteenth-century English oak sideboard that Bernie Flynn had brought back from England a decade ago when he covered a summit meeting in London. The sideboard had been converted to a bar. Bernie had converted to Republican conservatism, and Charlotte had converted to three drinks in the afternoon and Catholicism. At least that was what David told Carol, and the conversation had tended to support his observations.

Carol folded her hands, which felt cold even to her, as

Bernie and David entered the room. Bernie was tall, workout lean, and winter tan. His hair was full and white. He looked every bit as camera-ready as he had for almost ten years before becoming an affiliate executive. The sleeves of Bernie's red sweater were pulled back. The collar of his shirt was open. His arm was around David, who was almost six inches shorter and ten pounds heavier.

"Carol," Bernie said, moving to her side with a show of large white teeth that were, indeed, his own. "I'm sorry. All my fault. We were talking business and . . ."

"We were talking replacements," said David seriously.

Carol's eyes met her husband's. She saw concern and question.

"What's wrong, Carol?"

"Just tired," she said. "We should go."

"Got your coats right here," said Charlotte, hurrying back into the room.

"Might be a good idea to check in with your doctor in the morning," Bernie said, helping her on with her fur coat. "You look . . ."

". . . very pregnant," David said, pulling on his Eddie Bauer jacket.

"I think I *will* call the doctor in the morning," Carol said.

David reached for her arm, but she took a quick step forward to hug Charlotte. They all moved to the apartment door and went into the hallway where the women moved ahead toward the elevator.

"None of my business," Bernie whispered, "but Carol doesn't look well."

"*Rosemary's Baby* syndrome," David whispered back. "She's a little ambivalent. Doctor says it's natural."

"And I say it's natural," Bernie said softly. "Charlotte came close to not having our last. Between you, me, and the one-too-many double Scotches I just had, she almost decided on an abortion, long before they were politically correct."

Ahead of them Charlotte was supporting Carol and whispering to her. Probably, David thought, revealing some small, confidential sin of her husband's. It had been an awkward evening. An evening of ambivalence with Bernie shifting from proud mentor to comically envious rival to potential underling.

David hadn't wanted to come. He had given Carol a list of last-minute excuses, the best of which was Carol's sixth month of pregnancy and a night of cheek-freezing cold. But Carol had insisted on going, had been willing, it seemed, to even fight about it when he insisted.

"It's the last time," she had said. "It's the right thing to do."

"You hate them," David had reminded her as they got ready to leave that evening.

"I dislike them," Carol had corrected, hands trembling.

"Look at you," David had insisted.

"Look at yourself," Carol had answered shrilly.

And then she regretted it. David had let himself go, though he was no less than forty. He had a little belly and his father's heavy, sad dark face.

"Let's hope the baby doesn't look like me," David had said bitterly.

Carol had laughed.

"What's so funny?"

She had taken to laughing, crying at odd times for no reason that made sense to David. And it had gotten worse as Carol grew more and more obviously pregnant. David's mother had assured him that this was not abnormal. His aunt Esther had assured him. Doctor Saper had assured him, but it made David feel no better.

The elevator eased to a halt and the doors opened.

"We had a great time," David said, shaking Bernie's hand. "I won't forget all you've done for me and taught me."

"And I know you'll make me proud of you," Bernie said.

"Come on guys," Charlotte said. "The lady's tired."

David joined his wife in the elevator, faced forward with a smile, and watched the doors close on Charlotte and

Bernie, whose arm was around his wife's shoulder, hugging her close to him.

"What a man," David said. "Everyone knows he's *shtupping* Betty the receptionist, who's young enough to be his granddaughter. And there he stands. Big-city Gothic."

"Maybe he needs to be appreciated as a man," Carol said.

"Carol. Wrong is wrong. Family is family."

"Bertrand Russell, Immanuel Kant?" Carol said.

"You O.K., Carol?" David asked, taking his wife's arm as she tottered backward a step as the elevator dropped.

"I'll be fine," she said as the elevator bounced to a stop and the doors opened to the lobby.

"We don't need stoicism here, honey," David said, holding her. "The baby ..."

"The baby will be fine, David," she said. "The baby will be fine."

Raymond had known from the start that George was stupid. He was beginning to think that George might actually be feeble-minded like Jack-Jack Shorely's sister back on the island. She babble-babbled like George, sounded like she was making sense from a distance, but if you listened long enough you could start getting feeble-minded like her.

"Quiet," said Raymond.

"Got to keep everything working, mouth, feets, knees, neck or it gonna freeze," whined George. "Cold gonna kill me dead. Cold is no good for a big man. You ever see any fat Eskeemos?"

"I never see any Eskimos," said Raymond.

Inside the building he was watching, beyond the frosted windows, the doorman stood up and moved to the inside door. Two shapes inside, another couple.

"Eskimos look like Chinese," said George, squinting. "Like this. Only not."

The doorman opened the inner door and the couple stepped into the outer lobby, little more than a glassed-in square with a desk and phone for the doorman.

"Them," said Raymond.

George stopped shuffling and stepped to Raymond's side.

The couple was in their thirties, maybe. The man was not big, but he was bigger than the old man they had let pass and a lot younger.

"Why?" asked George.

"Look like he has got money," said Raymond, letting himself slide into the Islands patois he had struggled to lose. He wondered why he was doing it. To make George more comfortable? To make himself more comfortable with what he was about to do. "I know these things. Look at those coats. That's a fur she's wearing. You want to stand here all night? Maybe no one else come out for hours."

"No," said George, rocking as the doorman opened the outer door for the couple.

Raymond and George could here the couple thanking the doorman as a gasp of driving air hit the man and woman and pushed at the open door. The doorman put his shoulder to the door from the inside and closed it as the couple moved past the empty stone fountain in the circular driveway.

Boom-boom-boom. The gray-green dumpster clanged next to George's ears. Behind him waves hurled grating ice chunks and rage.

"Let's go," said Raymond.

Happy to be moving, thinking of someplace, anyplace warm, George almost knocked Raymond over as they stepped out of the rattling protective shadows of the dumpster.

Raymond looked back at the condo lobby. The doorman was sitting at his desk, a magazine open in front of him, one leg folded over the other.

"Slow," whispered Raymond. "Slow."

"I remember," George grunted.

The couple talked, but the two men could not hear what they were saying. The man said something and held the woman's hand. The woman sounded nervous. The man wore a jacket much like Raymond's, but this Eddie Bauer was new, clean, not a hand-me-down from who-knows-where. The jacket was nice, but it was the man's hat, one of those Russian fur hats, that fascinated George. The woman's head was uncovered except for the fuzzy white earmuffs. In the blue-white streetlights and the cold gray of the building windows, her hair looked like silver frost.

George looked down the street in both directions as Raymond held him back with a hand on his sleeve, giving the couple a twenty-yard lead. Raymond checked the doorman again. He was still looking at his magazine.

No one on the street now but the four of them and a slow sea of cars, see-no-evil cars moving past through the river of slush.

"They gettin' away," George whispered, trying to move ahead.

Raymond held the bigger man's sleeve.

"They goin' for their car, looks like," he said.

The couple, still talking, moved ahead slowly, the man's arm supporting the woman. The distance between the couple and the two men narrowed.

"Now, now, now," Raymond suddenly urged, and both men hurried forward.

George almost fell. He reached for the chill branches of a bare bush next to the building and kept himself erect.

Now the couple was next to the black metal gate of a fence around an old gray house, a holdout family home in the forest of high-rises. A brass plaque against the house identified it as the offices of J.W.R Ranpur, M.D., Cardiologist. There were no lights on in the home and office of Dr. Ranpur. Raymond had checked this only half an hour earlier. He had also checked to be sure the metal gate was open.

"Stop," Raymond said, stepping in front of the couple.

As he had been told to do, George moved close behind the man and woman, hovering over them.

The couple stopped.

Now Raymond, by the hazy light of a nearby streetlamp, could see the faces of his victims. The woman was pale, pretty, with a round, frightened face whose cheeks were chilled pink. The man, who seemed curious but not frightened, was short, a bit on the pudgy side. He wore glasses that were partly frosted along the upper rim.

"In here," said Raymond, opening the gate, watching to be sure no cars stopped.

It would, he hoped, look like nothing more than four people chatting in front of a house.

"What's going on?" asked the man.

Raymond removed his hand from his pocket and showed the pudgy man his gun, a gun he had bought only the day before for fifteen dollars and which he was not at all sure would fire.

"Step in there, man," he said, nodding through the gate. "You lose a few dollars and you and the lady go on."

"I don't . . ." the man started.

"Come on, come on here," George said, pulling out his own gun and shoving it into the back of the man with the Russian fur hat. George wanted that hat. But more than the hat he wanted to be out of there.

"David," the woman said, "do it. Give them your wallet."

"Not out here," Raymond hissed, looking back over his shoulder. "Get through the gate, man."

With George following close behind, the woman pulled at the arm of the man with the hat, and they edged through the gate.

Frozen grass crunched under George's feet as he pushed the man and woman toward the shadows of Dr. Ranpur's house.

"I'll give it to you," said David. "Let's not panic here."

"No one is panicking, man," said Raymond, looking toward the house and then the street. "Just don't give trouble."

"Come on, come on," George said, reaching up to remove his hat and shoving it in his pocket before yanking the man's hat from his head and putting it on his own. The hat was just a little too small and gave him an instant head-ache. But it was warm.

Without a hat the white man in front of him looked younger than George had thought him, even though the man's hair was getting thin. He reminded George of some actor.

"Take what you want," David said, holding one hand protectively in front of Carol and reaching into the pocket under his jacket with the other. "Just don't touch her. She's going to . . ."

"Touch . . . ? What you think we are?" asked George indignantly. "You think we gonna rape your woman out here like on an iceberg? What you think we are?"

Raymond took the wallet from David and shoved it into the frayed pocket of his blue ski jacket.

"Shut up," he said.

Carol let out a small sound like an island dove and her bareheaded husband took her in his arms.

"David," she said softly, "Please . . . "

"Don't you be saying that in front of these people," said George, facing Raymond. "Don't you be putting me down like you some kind of boss man."

"Fur," said Raymond, pointing his gun at the woman.

"She'll . . . " David began.

"Then you just give her your Eddie Bauer," said Raymond. "Better yet: I give her my Eddie Bauer and take yours."

Carol was whimpering now as she pulled away from David and began to take off the fur.

"No," said David.

George stepped forward, pushed David back, and pulled the fur coat to his chest the instant Carol had taken it off. Soft, cool fur brushed gently against his cheek.

"We got no time for this," said Raymond.

David took a step toward his wife, lost his footing, and crashed into the front steps of the office-home of J.W.R. Ranpur. His knee hit wood with a chill thump and crack.

Carol screamed. Without her fur, she looked pitiful, not

cold, in a blue-and-white dress that hung on her like one of George's mother's shifts.

"Shit," said George. "She gonna have a baby."

And then, as David pulled himself up from the steps, George heard the snap of a hammer against rock. Carol screamed again as David staggered back and sat spread-legged on the stairs.

Cars rushed by. Lake waves battered the shore behind the house. George thought he heard the clang-boom of the rusting green dumpster and then the sound of hammer and rock again. The man called David was sprawled on the steps now, his Eddie Bauer stained with black splotches, and George understood. Raymond had shot the man.

George felt a rush of warm imagined air from the beach of his childhood and the pain of the hat's tightness on his head. His eyes met Raymond's, and George was afraid of what he saw.

"Let's go," said Raymond. "George, you hear, let's go."

George didn't move. He turned to the woman, whose eyes were wide with terror. Her mouth was open and she couldn't catch her breath. The way she looked at him. Oh, the way she looked. She would haunt him. He knew that. She would haunt them both.

Raymond pulled the big man's sleeve.

"Let's go," he commanded.

George looked at the man sprawled on the steps and then at the crying woman in the blue dress, her head moving from side to side with fear in the winter chill. He could not live with that look.

George was not fully aware of what he did next. His body, his arms, his hands did what they were commanded, but the orders came from something slithering beneath his skin in the bloodred caverns of his skull.

George fired at the accusing woman. His gun was bigger than Raymond's, much bigger. He fired only once, but it sat the woman down, open-mouthed, surprised. She looked up, not at George who had shot her, but at Raymond, who turned suddenly on George, his gun leveled at the bigger man's chest.

"You crazy bastard," Raymond screamed. "The baby."

The two men stood over the bodies in the chill of Dr. Ranpur's ice-covered yard, their weapons raised at each other's chest for heartbeats upon heartbeats. And then Raymond pocketed his gun, looked at the woman, and took a step toward her, gun leveled in her direction. He let out a small, tortured cry as her bloody hands reached toward him and she spoke. Raymond turned and leaped over the black iron gate, almost losing his glasses. George didn't want to look back, but he couldn't stop himself. A light went on in the house, a light that seemed to drench the front yard. And George saw clearly what they had done. The man called David, looking bewildered, wisps of yellow-white hair quivering in the night wind, sat there, dead. The woman just sat looking up at him in her blue-and-white dress.

Perhaps she screamed or spoke, but George could hear nothing but the senseless steel-drum sound of the winter night. Hugging the fur to his face, he pushed open the gate and ran after Raymond, who was a gray running ghost far ahead of him in the mist.

BLACK KNIGHT IN RED SQUARE

A Pulitzer-winning American journalist is poisoned to death at the Moscow Film Festival, along with two Soviet businessmen and a Japanese visitor—all on the same night, in the same hotel. An international organization of terrorists has launched its most murderous offensive against both East and West. Foreigners continue dying at an alarming rate, in a huge embarrassment the Kremlin can ill afford. Chief Inspector Rostnikov leads the hunt for a dark-eyed woman of mystery and one very powerful bomb. The trail will take him, along with Karpo and Tkach, to the Soviet Union's most hallowed monument and the terrorists' ultimate target.

STUART KAMINSKY

A COLD RED SUNRISE

At an icebound naval weather station in far Siberia, two grisly murders are committed. Inspector Porfiry Rostnikov is dispatched to solve **one** of the murders, but he is not to solve the other killing even if the two are linked. In a single, fateful day, Rostnikov will hear two confessions, watch someone die, conspire against the government, and nearly meet his own death. All under the watchful eye of the KGB and someone closer and infinitely more terrifying.

Winner of the Edgar Award for Best Mystery Novel

DEATH OF A DISSIDENT

For Inspector Rostnikov, the investigation of the dissident Granovsky's murder should be easy. He will simply discover who plunged the rusty sickle into the dissident's chest. Rostnikov almost wishes the investigation won't turn out to be so simple. Before the case is over, Rostnikov will remember that wish and regret it.

STUART KAMINSKY

A FINE RED RAIN

Someone is killing the stars of the New Moscow Circus, and the bloody show must be stopped. A deadly stalker threatens the prostitutes of the city. Moscow's top cops take the case as multiple murders sweep the city. Rostnikov was once a great hero in the war against fascism, but too many clashes with the KGB have led to his demotion. And it's up to Rostnikov and his associates to stop the fine red rain of terror that has descended upon Moscow.

DEATH OF A RUSSIAN PRIEST

When Rostnikov arrives in the town of Arkush, he finds a community stunned by the murder of the outspoken Father Merhum. The priest's cryptic last words make Rostnikov wonder if this was a political assassination or a homegrown murder. Meanwhile, back in Moscow, Rostnikov's other associates are searching for an Arab girl everyone wants but no one can find. They find themselves in the seedy world of the Moscow night life, following the cold trail of the missing girl and the bloody tracks of a cunning killer.

RED CHAMELEON

A long Russian summer brings crime in Moscow to a deadly boil. The violent and inexplicable murder of an old man in his bathtub and the theft of a worthless candlestick send Inspector Porfiry Rostnikov on a hunt into the past. But as his search narrows down to one feared and elusive man, the trail winds back to the most unexpected and dangerous place for Inspector Rostnikov.

STUART KAMINSKY

ROSTNIKOV'S VACATION

Under orders from his superior, Rostnikov leaves the city for some time off to stroll by the seashore, tend to his recuperating wife, and read American crime novels. When a vacationing fellow officer meets with a mysterious demise, Rostnikov suddenly finds himself unofficially back on the job and on the trail of a murderer. And if his hunch is correct, the powerful winds of change in Russia have begun to carry the ugly smell of conspiracy straight to the steps of the Kremlin.

———◆———

Also by Stuart Kaminsky:

LIEBERMAN'S FOLLY

Sixty-year-old Chicago police detective Abe Lieberman has his share of troubles. His partner drinks too much, and his boss is an ogre. Enter Estralda Valdez, a stunning Mexican prostitute who comes to Lieberman with a problem of her own. This "problem" leads to a murder that will plunge Lieberman into the darkest depths of Chicago crime and corruption, and might just get him killed.

STUART KAMINSKY